Nicolas Verdan was born in Vevey, Switzerland in 1971. He was a prominent journalist before turning full-time to fiction. He shares his time between Switzerland and Greece. He won a number of literary prizes in Switzerland and France for his previous novels, and *The Greek Wall* is his first work available in English.

THE GREEK WALL

Nicolas Verdan

Translated from the French
by W. Donald Wilson

BITTER LEMON PRESS
LONDON

BITTER LEMON PRESS
First published in the United Kingdom in 2018 by
Bitter Lemon Press, 47 Wilmington Square, London WC1X 0ET

www.bitterlemonpress.com

First published in French as *Le Mur Grec* by
Bernard Campiche Éditeur, Orbe, 2015

The translation of this work was supported by
the Swiss Arts Council Pro Helvetia

A CIP record for this book is available from the British Library
ISBN 978–1–908524–850
eBook ISBN 978–1–908524–867

swiss arts council
prohelvetia

Typeset by Tetragon, London
Printed and bound by CPI Group (UK) Ltd, Croydon CR0 4YY

Often on my travels I have been in peril from rivers, in peril from brigands, in peril from those of my own nation, in peril from pagans, in peril in cities, in peril in deserts, in peril on the sea, in peril from false brethren.

(2 CORINTHIANS 11: 26)

Glossary

17N: A Greek terrorist group, the Revolutionary Organization 17 November, which assassinated Stephen Saunders, the British military attaché in Athens, on 8 June 2000.

Baglamas: A musical instrument with plucked strings.

Çifetelli: A dance of Turkish origin, still found throughout countries that were once part of the Ottoman Empire.

Colonel's Regime: The series of right-wing military juntas that governed Greece from 1967 to 1974.

Egnatia Odos: Also known as the Via Egnatia, the Egnatia Odos was a Roman road running from what is now Durrës, in Albania, across northern Greece and into Turkey. A modern motorway across northern Greece (the A2, part of the European E90) is commonly called by the same name.

Episodia: A political demonstration accompanied by violent and destructive incidents.

Evros: The Greek name of the river Maritsa (or Meriç in Turkish), which runs through Bulgaria and then forms the land frontier between Greece and Turkey. It gives its name to the surrounding region.

Evzone: A soldier of the presidential guard, dressed in traditional uniform.

Gaida: A Greek bagpipe.

Great Catastrophe: After the fall of the Ottoman Empire following World War I, Kemal Atatürk led a Turkish war of liberation to prevent the dismemberment of Turkey by some major European powers and Greece. This resulted in the expulsion of much of the substantial Greek population of Asia Minor, including the burning of the Greek districts of Smyrna (now Izmir), and in many deaths.

KKE: Kommunistiko Komma Elladas, the Communist Party of Greece, founded in 1918.

New Democracy: The main centre-right political party in Greece, founded in 1974 by Konstantinos Karamanlis. It won a majority in the general elections of 2004 and 2007 and entered into coalitions with PASOK between 2011 and 2015.

PASOK: Panellínio Sosialiwtikó Kínima, the Panhellenic Socialist Movement, is the Greek Social Democratic Party. It won a majority in the election of 2009 and entered into coalitions with New Democracy between 2011 and 2015.

Pomaks: A Muslim community living in Greece, the Pomaks are of Slavic origin (hence a minority among the Turkish Muslim minority in Greece). They are thought to be the descendants of converts to Islam under the Ottoman occupation of Bulgaria. Their language is a dialect of Bulgarian, though under Turkish influence many have also acquired Turkish. A mufti is a spiritual and secular leader.

Tavli: A Greek variety of backgammon.

Troika: The European Commission, International Monetary Fund, and European Central Bank.

Prologue

In normal circumstances he'd have gone on his way, paying no attention to the neon sign suspended in the moonless sky above the river. But at this moment, in the depth of night, the unexpected encounter with the word "Eros" strikes him like a portent. This is where the colonel has arranged to meet him. He turns off the engine and parks his rental car on the verge. The car that has been following him for the past twenty minutes or so has also stopped, but he doesn't notice. Alone more than ever, he only has eyes for those pink letters, which seem at the cost of their meaning to spell out a recipe for unhappiness. At the moment, he no longer knows why he is here in this spot alongside a national highway, outside this brothel on the very edge of the Schengen Area. Perhaps, instead of discussing the wall inside, he might find a body like Christina's? Not her face, no, he wouldn't recognize it in that place. 'But maybe her perfume? Just a woman's perfume, a scent, just her scent, please, please tell me if there mightn't be, here in this place, in the countryside, on the frontier of Europe, a girl wearing Rykiel Woman. Who knows, maybe a young woman, here, on this road to the north? I'd like to find a woman with her figure, with Christina's substance, with that resilient quality of hers, with Christina's earthy attraction, always resilient yet thrown back, the fall of Christina's body, solid flesh in which to spill yourself.'

Which way to the entrance? On the side facing the river the brothel's exterior is dark and windowless. Exploring to the right of the building, he comes to a deserted car park. Could the entrance be hidden on its western side? Suddenly impatient to enter the Eros, he retraces his steps and skirts the brothel in the opposite direction, failing to notice an exterior passageway leading to the door. Then he feels a glacial caress across his brow, the sudden contact of an icy chill that takes his breath away and makes him stumble. Suffocating in the smell of laundry, it takes him a few seconds to realize that he has become entangled in some large, wet sheets hung out to dry in front of the building. Freeing himself of the brothel's clammy embrace, he tries to stand up, but his left knee doesn't respond. A light seems to have gone on; he must have made a noise. Anyway, now that the terrace is lit up he can see his shadow limping on the concrete surface where the stained, crumpled sheets lie twisted.

A light fixed to the wall has come on; someone has switched it on, they are coming, she is coming, a young woman walking towards him, looking quite through him so that he doesn't quite see her advancing towards him; at first he sees only her wide-open eyes and his reflection in them, he sees himself standing in her field of vision, but then he notices the axe the young woman is holding. As her face draws closer he sees himself more clearly in her eyes and suddenly takes stock of his situation: she considers him an obstacle, a looming impediment, he is an obstruction in the young woman's dark-veiled eyes, an obstacle she must remove from her path in order to see behind him, gazing towards a vanishing point, and it suddenly it occurs to him that he had better get out of her way – fend her off, duck, dodge, sidestep her.

But the axe is already poised, suspended, all the more menacing in that its mass rests on the young woman's shoulders, leaving her no choice but to unleash all the accumulated violence in the muscles of her lifted arms.

In the instant that follows, only a "No!" comes to his lips. Then something appears behind him, another presence in the eyes of the young woman – who is very young as far as he can tell in the fraction of a second in which she brings down the axe – and he cries out in Greek, "No! No!"

Someone – a man or a woman? – someone thinks, 'Silence falls on the frontier, where now only the rolling river Evros flows.'

Episode I

The street rises and falls like a wave, surges again, swells, and falls again. These undulations give a sense of the neighbourhood, with its crests and hollows, its gentle slopes. It is a street leading into the city, when this story begins, once upon a time, at two in the morning, on a densely populated hill, on the night of 21 and 22 December 2010, on Irakleous Street, in Neos Kosmos, Athens, Greece.

'What does a severed head look like?' wonders Agent Evangelos.

He is standing in the street facing the Batman, a bar diminished by everything about itself: the green phosphorescence of its sign, the cheap alcohol it serves and its regulars, all participants in the death of a world, still devoted to the songs of yesteryear, and their youth pinned up on the wall – a photo of Theodorakis, a view of the Acropolis taken from the terrace of the Galaxy (another bar, on the twelfth floor of the Hilton), the faded colours of Greek summers on ads from the 1970s, and the round yellow sun on Olympic Airways posters. Every evening in Athens, the Batman's customers carry on as if nothing had changed, although so much is dead and gone and despite all the pitfalls that await, the menace outside, beyond the window of the bar, on this street where Agent Evangelos is standing, uncertain about what to do next.

If there hadn't been that phone call, that conversation with his colleague – with that severed head to blame for it all – this story would have been very different, it wouldn't have taken the same form, would have been impossible to relate, have had neither head nor tail – ouch! He'd have ordered another drink and sat with his eyes closed listening to Kazantzidis; and if he had waited a little longer he would have been joined by Irena, the owner of the only jazz club in the capital worthy of the name.

When she comes to the Batman, Irina makes her appearance around 1.30, accompanied by a few musicians, an employee and her barman, an entourage drawn along in the turbulent wake of a ferry to the islands. Not for anything in the world would she miss an "after", as she calls it, rolling the "r".

Agent Evangelos likes Irina, her plump figure, her outrageous assertions, her inexhaustible affections, her generous love for the masculine gender – a generosity of being that turns her corpulence into a distinction. It would have been a different story, set here in the Batman, but very soon Agent Evangelos must be on his way. He goes back inside, for he has left his jacket on a hook under the bar. He pays what he owes, and leaves.

'What does a head severed from the body look like?' he wonders. A phone call has come; he must leave immediately.

Just a few more minutes and Agent Evangelos might have encountered Irina. That approaching sound of an engine is she; with one finger she manoeuvres the four-by-four, which has just stopped in front of the Batman. The passengers on the rear seat look out; all of them have seen the same things: glimpses of the city, the confused message of the streets, voiceless graffiti on the filmstrip of the walls, the weight of lowered shop blinds, the greenish glow from the forest of balconies, the squashed oranges on the asphalt, flattened candle flames. They have seen all of it go by, but driving along they passed no remark.

Athens is their capital city, but they are not from here. They are Greek citizens, but they have Turkish names. Onstage this evening they sang in both languages: the language of their origin and the language of their pass-port. In administrative terms, they belong to the Turkish minority in Thrace. Words on an official stamp identify them as foreigners in their own land. Opposite that wall only their music rings true, and the public is aware of it. The applause was thunderous and sincere – a polite way, in other words, to conceal the uneasiness inspired by these Greeks who are not entirely Greek.

By the time Irena pushes open the door to the Batman, Agent Evangelos is already in his car. He has turned onto the first street on the right, a one-way toboggan slope that drags the high-rises of Neos Kosmos down with it until they encounter the crash barriers on Kallirois Avenue. At the intersection, the traffic lights flicker and turn green.

The taxis, catapulted up towards the city centre, assail the wall of the former Fix brewery with a fusillade of headlight beams. The abandoned plant is still intended to become the Museum of Contemporary Art, though the cultural future to which it is promised is in no hurry to materialize. Athens has run out of euros, and the concrete behemoth sits deserted, hemmed in by traffic.

On the other side, the multiple lanes of Syngrou Avenue, linking the city to the coast, are flanked by large hotels of glass and steel, and striptease joints. Driving towards Faliro, ablaze with lights like the overnight ferry to Crete, Piraeus to Chania, a twelve-hour crossing, scheduled to arrive in the early hours, imagining a siren blast in the muted torpor of the eucalyptus and perspiring pines; at the end of the quay a tanker with flat tyres, always the same dog nosing through the scattered remnants of a spilled load of tomatoes, twelve hours after the ferry's left, about to close its loading doors with an articulated lorry appearing with a roar from behind a warehouse; a minute to go, with the ship's propellers already stirring up the silt in basin E3.

To his right the headquarters of the New Democracy party are all lit up, a ponderous, unmanageable vessel. In the grandiose entrance hall a lounging security guard has lost interest in the giant screen on which a formidable army of men in suits and ties processes in an endless loop, shaking hands on the triumphant worksites of a Greece sold off bit by bit to Chinese and Emirates capital while the European Union lags behind with its Siemens factories, Casino supermarkets and H&M clothing stores.

Then comes the black hole of a building long under construction, and then, on the sinister upper floors of commercial buildings with opaque windows, endless voids of office space awaiting tenants.

Finally, there seems to be an opportunity to turn onto Kallirois Street when a Pakistani face appears beyond the windscreen. Agent Evangelos is startled. He waves the window-washer away and then launches his vehicle across Syngrou Avenue. Usually he'll give them a coin or two, but this evening, though he doesn't really know why, he felt like punching the fellow armed with bucket and squeegee in the face.

Agent Evangelos listens to himself as he drives. His movements resound inside him, the external noise has permeated him, rumbling in his temples. A wave of weariness sweeps over him. Soon he'll be in the plane to Alexandroupolis as it makes the wide turn over Attica, the sea filling the aircraft window, the island of Chios on the tilting horizon – could that forest of wind turbines be Euboea? Skiathos ahead, the Gulf of Volos below with its seafood tavernas, tablecloths with their crude maps of Greece printed in blue, the Macedonian wine in a copper jug, a gust of wind from the sea emptying the ashtrays, all of Greece, the orchards on Mount Pelion, seat 14D, Aegean Airlines, a private company, 31 Viltanioti Street, Kifissia, Athens 14564, twenty-nine planes, a fleet of twenty-two Airbus A320, four Airbus A321 and three Airbus A319, shares on the rise, new route to Azerbaijan recently introduced; his plane flying at cruising speed over a landscape of mountains and islands; the descent has already begun.

It glides over Samothrace, a rock emerging from the Aegean, a sheer, vertical cliff face, a rising vertigo, a steep shoreline marked by a thick streak of foam, a white garter stitched to the dry land; but then it's the sea again, as if the Thracian coast will never come into view.

Shouldn't he be able to see the Evros delta already? Agent Evangelos will certainly find out tomorrow. He knows he's awaited on the bank of the river. In Alexandroupolis, the head of the regional section of the National Intelligence Service will be in the parking lot of Democritus Airport to meet him, but he has no idea what the man looks like.

His eyes are stinging; it is too hot in the car, and Agent Evangelos opens the window. Why did he close it? It's true, that Pakistani had a strange look about him; Evangelos didn't like his eyes.

'What does a severed head look like?' he wonders. He can still hear his colleague on the phone: "They've found a dead body."

"Yes, I know, you said so already, but dead bodies are two-a-penny every week along the Evros, so please tell me why you're calling at this hour of the night to let me know?"

"That dead body's assigned to us."

I think that in that moment I was angry. "Is this a joke or what? Since when have we been going off to the border to fish for dead bodies? There are illegals dying every week trying to cross the Evros."

"Yes, but the police in Orestiada say this body's different."

Silence. The next question was inevitable: "What's so special about this one?"

"All they've found is the head."

Agent Evangelos asked his colleague to repeat what he'd just said, as the music was loud. There isn't another bar like the Batman in all of Athens. That was where he'd finally found what he'd been seeking for months: an atmosphere like before the crisis. The bar is nothing but a narrow bottleneck with a high ceiling, enforcing sociability and offering an ideal repair for those who, like Evangelos, have resisted the first austerity measure imposed on the Greeks by Brussels: a general ban on smoking in public establishments.

In the smoke-filled Batman blackened lungs could breathe the air of freedom. Agent Evangelos has given up smoking. But his grandfather once owned a tobacconist's shop in Smyrna, and he can still hear him describing, between coughing fits, how he used to plunge his fist into the bales of Macedonian tobacco and sniff it before pointing at the one that met with his approval.

The moment Agent Evangelos stepped outside the Batman he regretted having left his jacket inside. A cold wind laden with moisture from the sea made his voice catch as he asked his colleague to go over everything from the beginning.

"The police in Orestiada have found a head, you say?"

"Yes, on the bank of the Evros, near the marshes."

"A head, all by itself? What about the rest, the body?"

"Nothing, sir. Just a head, in Orestiada, found beside the river."

"But who found it?"

"A Frontex patrol."

"What kind of patrol, exactly?"

"You know, surely: the European Agency's frontier guards responsible for patrolling the borders…"

"Yes, I get that, but who was it exactly? What country's police did they come from? The French? The Dutch?"

"No, no, they were Finns, I think. They were patrolling with their Alsatian when it suddenly got all excited."

Until the creation of the Schengen Area in 1997 each country was responsible for its own borders. That all changed in 2004, when the Olympic Games were held in Greece.

'All the fault of that damned Amsterdam Treaty, allowing free movement of citizens between member states,' Agent Evangelos often tells himself, doubtful as he is of the effectiveness of police and judicial cooperation in combating illegal immigration.

"Don't we already have an officer on the spot in Thrace who can look into it?" asks Agent Evangelos.

"Yes, he's spending the night in Orestiada."

"But if I understand properly, his presence isn't enough?"

"Well, actually, as I was saying, sir, this isn't a run-of-the-mill fatality."

"Just get to the facts, good God!"

"The head, the guy, well, the head, the dead man, well, he's not a migrant."

"What are you trying to tell me?"

"That's what the police captain in Orestiada says."

"He says what? Just come out with it, for God's sake!"

"He says it's not an illegal, and it's a suspicious death."

"Well, of course it's suspicious! And what allows him to say it's not an illegal?"

"Because it looks like a Westerner."

"And what does a Westerner look like, according to you?"

"Like a European, like a Greek, I don't know. Our officer on the spot is of the same opinion."

"It's because you think you look like a European, is that it? And what about me, have you ever seen my eyebrows, my dark complexion? A European! So what?"

"I don't know, sir, but in Orestiada they're saying that the case is over their heads; they say it's for Athens. It's for us."

Agent Evangelos knows that his colleague is right. It would take less than a decapitation in a military zone on the Greco-Turkish border to alert Directorate C of the National Intelligence Service, the branch responsible for counter-espionage, counterterrorism and organized crime. And the matter of looks makes no difference. Illegal or not, this head seems likely to raise a stink around the frontier question. Greece has already been accused of doing a poor job in the Evros delta. How many illegals manage to cross the river every day? Two hundred, three hundred?

Several European countries, such as France, have accused Greece of allowing too many migrants across the border with Turkey. President Nicolas Sarkozy has even said that a country that can't control its borders should be excluded from the Schengen Area.

A severed head. They'll have to look for the body. The reverse would have been more difficult, of course. But Agent Evangelos will have to deal with his fatigue, a recent phenomenon, along with his tendency to view everything in context and his ability to procrastinate.

It's true that three years from now he'll be turning in his badge. A well-deserved retirement, as they used to say when you could be sure of getting your pension. But nowadays, with the crisis…

The crisis… a word Agent Evangelos finds it difficult to utter. The debt crisis. Words that fail to explain how Greece has been reduced to this. Wasn't it just in 2007 that the mandarins of the International Monetary Fund said that the Greek economy had "made remarkable strides"? Evangelos can still hear the first head of the Central European Bank, Wim someone or other… Yes, Wim Duisenberg. Hadn't he said in the early 2000s that Greece's economic performance was "admirable, remarkable"? They almost pointed to Greece as a model of growth. 'And then,' he remembers, 'one October morning we woke with a bad taste in our mouths.' Agent Evangelos can still hear George Papandreou's voice as he announced to the Greeks that their right-wing government had been cooking the books. "The truth is," he had said, "that our country is deeper in debt than you have been told." Everyone in the country knows what came next. Athens called on the help of the good doctors from the IMF and the European Commission approved Papandreou's austerity plan, placing Greece under close oversight. The euro nosedived, and Greece with it. There followed a succession of European rescue plans, and the Greeks demonstrated in the streets. The great international moneybags was called to the rescue. In Germany, Chancellor Angela Merkel adopted a tougher tone: Germans couldn't be expected to pay higher taxes to bail out the wastrels in southern Europe. It was a crisis. 'The crisis,' thinks Evangelos. 'Maybe that's why every day feels so overwhelming? The fact you have to search endlessly for words to describe what's wrong.' Something's not right; there's a sick feeling in the pit of Evangelos's stomach – maybe the sixty-something crisis? 'The crisis, the crisis everywhere. No, it's something else. For a year or two now, since the start of the crisis... No! For a year or two, ever since petrol went up to over two euros a litre, since my salary was reduced by a good quarter, since I've seen little old men poking through the bins in front of my apartment building, since...'

Why does Agent Evangelos keep looking beyond his constant nausea? 'No, it's with myself that something has gone wrong. And it has nothing to do with the present chaos. Nothing to do with Merkel, nor the Troika, as they call the IMF, Brussels, and the World Bank, all the banks bought out and sold out, and the politicians sold out with them, and on top of it the directorate requiring all the agents to pay for coffee out of their own pockets.'

He can't say when it began, but Evangelos feels the angst welling up in him. 'And this dull fear affecting me like a beta blocker.'

Orders are issued: A severed head on the banks of the Evros; a crime on the Schengen frontier. Alert! Emergency meeting, reports, ministerial orders, make telephone calls, make contacts on site, organize the personnel in Thrace, get there by plane, first a debriefing with the top military command, maps of the zone, files, what's the name of the officer responsible for the Evros region? Who knows how the head was found? Establish relations with the media in case there's a leak, ask Ria who works in the head office of Public Relations to clamp down and let nothing get out.

Have the Turks been informed? Who'll oversee communications with Frontex, that goddamn agency with its headquarters in Warsaw? Alert! Agent Evangelos must go, he hasn't any choice.

And always the same angst. But when did it start? A weary feeling that drains his energy. Evangelos can see his familiar landscape changing: the filthy windows of the agency building that never get cleaned. And that persistent rumour of drastic reductions in personnel.

Evangelos thinks this matter of the severed head bodes him no good. They'll hold the slightest misstep against him. In the meantime, he has to get organized. He has a plane to catch tomorrow, and he must establish a list of the people to contact on his arrival in Thrace, a thousand kilometres from Athens. He has no appetite for this.

Agent Evangelos gets a grip on himself. 'What's the explanation? What's the hang-up? Why the resistance?

The thing is, I don't want anything to do with this severed head! But why? Because memories return. Yes, that's it, old memories returning: dawn, an island, a harbour. No choice but to obey, and ask no questions. No connection whatsoever: that was forty years ago. Where's the link?'

He stops searching; Evangelos knows why he is feeling so weary: it's his sense of déjà vu. For years he thought he could forget the whole business, block it out. 'Yet today, with all that's going on in the country, I have to try twice as hard to forget about it, now that it all seems about to happen again. Those raised arms in the slums, the militia hunting down emigrants, and the directorate continuing to target anarchists. It's odd; nowadays it's not men in masks heading for Syntagma Square to attack Parliament.'

There are no more rockets fired at the banks, no more Molotov cocktails setting the streets of the capital on fire. Why aren't there more street demonstrations? So much anger – the white-hot metal sheath of the Christmas tree reduced to ashes on Syntagma Square, the stones thrown at the police, Stadiou Street in flames, the strategic retreat behind the railings of the Polytechnic, the fading anger. There's no one left to be surprised.

"I'm so dog-tired," he sighs.

But Agent Evangelos will travel to the border. He'll do his job.

He'll leave tomorrow; in the meantime, he'll go somewhere else. The shortest route is the Sacred Way, and if it wasn't for that train he'd be there already.

Where?

Agent Evangelos would be there already, if it wasn't for that level-crossing bell. He'd already have reached the big intersection and driven under the ring-road bridge before heading diagonally through Peristeri, the great western suburb that rises ungracefully to the stark slopes of Mount Aigaleo.

A moment later, the barriers come down. A long horn blast announces a goods train. Agent Evangelos can see the outline of the driver inside the cabin of the diesel locomotive, which is followed by an endless succession of graffiti-covered wagons, its clatter sawing the city in two.

There's not a soul to be seen this evening in this quarter full of former warehouses where the only stocks of merchandise are relics of Greek pop music: faces with make-up and gelled hair frozen on huge, outdated concert posters, and the trampled carnations on the stage at three in the morning when the dancing is done, when Parios and his group always ended by playing the *nisiotika*, the songs from the islands – Parios, the little king of Naxos, playing it up the way he would in his village every 15 August, except that here a bottle of whisky costs three hundred euros. But this evening, outside, at the dead street-corners, the wasteland car parks are empty. The *bouzoukia* have closed, and that little gang only sing and dance on invitation – open-air concert tomorrow, free for the good people, the obligatory party in the private amphitheatre of some ship owner, his way of buying the right to take off five times a day in his helicopter, he takes off and lands, he takes off from some bald pebble in the Cyclades on which he has set down his villa. Everybody to the port this evening, it's the rich guy's treat! A good guy, there's not a word you can say against him: thousand-euro gifts at baptisms, a gift of new windows for the village school, and the fish in the taverna yesterday evening too. This generous individual's yacht is anchored in the dark water of the little inlet. It flies the Australian ensign. What a patriot!

And in the meantime, on the Sacred Way, in front of the deserted club, only the roasted-corn vendor tries to keep up appearances. He turns his corn like on Friday evenings, when the avenue becomes an amusement park with its merry-go-round of four-by-fours in front of the club entrances.

Where is he off to now, Agent Evangelos?

Agent Evangelos isn't on his way home; he's not going to sleep in his own bed, on Makriyanni Street. He is heading directly west; he simply knows that he has the keys with him. He always has, since his parents died.

From the outside the house is the same as ever. Inside, he has gutted it completely. It's an empty shell, like a cradle with only the frame remaining, not even a smell. Where is he going? He is going home. He feels at home there, which isn't surprising, since he has made a clean sweep inside: not a single memory remains; there's nothing to remind him of his childhood; it really is somewhere new. But then why did he keep it? He could have sold it, replaced it with a four-storey apartment building. No, he has kept his parents' house as it was out of reverence for the view, with its panorama of Athens, a spot from where he can measure the city's evolution. Four walls and a flat roof built by his father, a rampart to protect him from himself.

If Agent Evangelos had demolished his parents' house he would have lived with its memory. He would have missed it, and that would have recalled pictures of his childhood, but if he had left it just as it was he would also have been overwhelmed by nostalgia. He had preferred to make it his lookout. From the heights of Petroupolis, sitting on the terrace, Agent Evangelos can see the city's rise and fall, he can feel it vibrate. To see Athens evolve you need a stationary viewpoint. We always consider things from the same vantage point. Adopting a new one means condemning yourself to refuse change. But change inhabits us all.

And, when he considers Athens, Evangelos no longer thinks of anything. His parents are dead and gone; his mother died ten years ago, taken by cancer, long before his father. He had lasted much longer. He'd died in January of this year, in his eighty-ninth year. He was born in Smyrna, in 1922, the year of the great calamity, when Atatürk's troops drove the Greek population into the sea.

But is that really the history of his family? His own history?

Agent Evangelos isn't too sure any more. After long weeks spent wandering the islands and the first Greek ports on the mainland, his grandparents had existed for months and years in hardship and poverty. Evangelos knows the story off by heart: ruined financially, meeting hostility in a mother country that viewed them as Easterners with peculiar customs, they had to create a place of their own. For a long time they lived in a shack in Nea Ionia, an inhospitable landscape far from the city centre, in what was for years a refugee camp, a herd of white canvas tents amid an expanse of wild grasses.

Agent Evangelos knows what came next: his father grew up in poverty. He found a job as a page in the Hotel Grande Bretagne shortly before the Nazis entered Athens. In the 1950s, not long after Evangelos was born, he was promoted to maître d'hôtel. By 1962 he had accumulated enough savings to build a little house on a stony, still uninhabited hillside directly west of Athens, in Petroupolis.

Agent Evangelos was ten when he moved there with his father, mother and grandmother. 'She lived with us for five years,' he repeats to himself. 'I'm pretty sure she died the year the Colonels seized power.'

The neighbourhood Agent Evangelos knew in his youth is unrecognizable today. Only the tiny house and its minuscule garden remain unchanged. In 1972, a developer tried to convince his father to sell him the land. He planned to demolish the house and erect an apartment building in its place. His father would have received two apartments in exchange.

'But my dad refused. He didn't want that.'

Almost forty years have passed. 'It's 2010, and what have you got?' Agent Evangelos asks himself. 'A severed head on the banks of a frontier river.' He launches his car into the labyrinth of one-way streets leading to the heights of Petroupolis. 'It's time to leave it behind, that whole history, Greece. Those refugees from Smyrna, from the Great Catastrophe, mean nothing to me any more. For too long

I thought my future had been compromised definitively by that exodus. I've had enough of the tortured history that's supposed to be ours as Greeks, and apparently my own. What an excuse! Our history books are poisonous, our songs and novels are filled with venom.

'Forget, I must forget the books and take up the story as I see it, not get involved in other people's memories. I have to learn a different language, change my vocabulary. My job is delving into earlier lives, spying on people's lives, the lives of the ones I interrogate, the ones I wiretap. Report, record, Agent Evangelos, but don't get involved. Keep out of it. Never discuss your private life! It's the motto of the National Intelligence Service.'

Evangelos has led several lives, and there's nothing to connect them. Their narratives are irreconcilable, which is why he tries never to talk about his past. Why would he want to remember his childhood? What's the use of evoking his teenage years? His education? His divorce? All so many successive, incompatible stories, a series of accidents of the kind we all experience and that finally get us lost if we try to reread them. 'Our lives are made of bits and pieces,' he murmurs. 'Trying to reconcile them means disassembling ourselves, agreeing to become other than what we are.'

Evangelos has never made public mention of the young man who was conscripted, compelled to enlist, on the double, on the docks one morning in August 1972. He was only twenty. 'How could you refuse?' At that age, you become a soldier, that's the way it has always been, standing at attention after getting off the ferry, chin raised, eyes fixed on the Turkish coast, so close, carrying a letter he'd started to write at sea in his canvas kitbag, expressing all his love for a girl who would soon, every morning of his existence, still be sleeping in another man's arms at this moment. The engines of the turning lorries, the end of a first life and the beginning of a new one beneath the walls of Kos, among shouted orders, and the boat for Athens already on its way, its hold still open.

The rasp of a handbrake being pulled, a car door slamming in the heights of Petroupolis: who but he, Evangelos, coming to park in front of the closed shutters? He has arrived. The gate creaks, the shadows of the terrace lengthen with his approach; there is no one else, just a passing motorbike. A TV glows somewhere upstairs in the nearby apartment building, an insomniac buzz leads to a dustbin lid that flaps in the breeze: all the silence of familiar sounds.

Before entering, he decides to go up onto the roof, using the exterior metal staircase. Every evening, before going to bed, in all seasons and in all weather, he likes to spend time up here.

Opposite, where military aerials wink on the long crest of Mount Hymettus, the landscape is shifting, profiled against a sky on which cottony strands scatter the first crimson hues of dawn.

It will be a beautiful day. North of the central plain of Attica, a vast wheelbarrow laden with shards of marble, Mount Pentelikon's bald pate bares its eastern side to the sun.

The mountainsides are so scorched that nothing remains to halt the thrust of the city, which has disturbed the soil so much that it seems to emerge from it like an ossuary.

Sunlight is already attacking the rear of the house. A cock crows in a makeshift henhouse on one of the bushy slopes that mark the city's edge. Evangelos returns to the little garden below, which is overgrown by weeds. It is time to get some rest. The scrape of the bolt against the strike plate of the glass-panelled door shatters the marble silence of the entrance hall. The blinds in the main room are drawn. Evangelos is on the sofa. His eyes are about to close when he feels a vibration. The phone in his jacket has lit up.

Andromeda, calling so early?

"Sweetheart, have you seen the time?"

"Dad! It's a daughter; she was born at three this morning!"

Agent Evangelos is a grandfather. Dawn is breaking over *Tsimentoupolis*, "Cement City", the name by which Athenians sometimes refer to their city.

The corridor ends at a large, very tall window. Agent Evangelos looks out. From that height, on the third floor of the maternity clinic, he can see beyond the hospital car parks that have pushed the last surviving marble works on Erithrou Stavrou Street into the background. Along what was once a side road in the countryside of Nea Filothei, a little 1950s house, surrounded by greenery, is the last remaining witness to a landscape formerly composed of olive groves and a few flat-roofed sheds surrounded by vegetable gardens which once marked the frontier with the wealthy neighbourhoods occupying the nearby heights of Filothei.

Agent Evangelos consults his watch. His flight to Alexandroupolis leaves at 3.30. He has a little time to spare. Giorgos is to drive him to Venizelos Airport. The Mitera Clinic is on the way. His colleague won't breathe a word about this unofficial stop. Agent Evangelos likes Giorgos a lot: he is a young father who would really have liked his wife to give birth there, in a private clinic. Held up in the traffic jams on Kifisias Avenue, he had made no comment when Agent Evangelos told him he had become a grandfather and would like to visit his daughter on the way. Giorgos understood perfectly, and accelerated down the long straight road across which a footbridge had been built. It had taken an accident on the pedestrian crossing, the death of a boy from Athens College high on drugs, for them to decide to do something at last. Until then the authorities had turned a deaf ear.

On Kifisias Avenue Giorgos said that his wife had had her baby in the military hospital. He'd have liked his wife to give birth in such a nice clinic. "We'd really have liked the Mitera Clinic," Agent Evangelos hears him say.

"The Mitera, the Mitera, a lovely clinic," repeats Giorgos as they are passing the bridge, the one at the crossroads for Chalandri, the spot where, in 2000, the 17N terrorist group shot the British military attaché Stephen Saunders. Agent Evangelos remembers the precise time: it was 7.45 a.m., he was right on the spot, as he'd just arrived on the bridge. Traffic was at a standstill, creating a huge traffic jam. The witnesses said they had seen two men on a motorbike, wearing helmets, one short and the other tall; the bike was an Enduro.

Agent Evangelos remembers it as if it was yesterday. The bullets were from a 7.62 mm Heckler and Koch G3. On the bridge, a shattered windscreen, the blood-soaked man in a white car, there on the bridge, nearly eleven years ago…

"Immediately after, you have to turn left! Giorgos?"

Giorgos takes the left turn without any problem. He catches on fast: the birth of his granddaughter, which way to go. As his colleague enters the congested street past the hospital, the radio announces the date of the early elections: "On 6 May, Greece will go to the polls."

"8 June," murmurs Agent Evangelos.

"No, 6 May," Giorgos corrects him.

"No, no, I was just thinking of something else." It was 8 June 2000, at 7.45. They'd got him. The Brit was soaking in his own blood. The cars were driving slowly by; it was already warming up by then.

"Not serious. By the way, I think you told me, and I should know, but how old are you? Sixty this year, is that it?" asked Giorgos.

Evangelos nodded, and Giorgos laughed aloud: "Young to be a granddad!"

Just now on the radio the prime minister had announced early elections and the weather forecast was predicting a hot day. Giorgos changed the station and lowered the window; he turned the radio off and slowed down as they passed the Hygeia, the polyclinic that precedes the maternity clinic. He stopped opposite some florists' shops, in front of the first of the taxis parked two abreast. The taxi driver unleashed a volley of insults and blew his horn, and Giorgos said again, "I'd really have liked my wife to have had the baby here."

"Wait for me, I'll be less than half an hour," says Agent Evangelos.

"Best wishes for the little one! I'll park a little farther on," Giorgos tells him, already moving off. Now Agent Evangelos can see him down the street, chatting with the attendant of the last car park. In no time they'll be sitting on plastic chairs under the awning of an old caravan, like two old friends side by side on a little wall beneath a plane tree, on a village square somewhere in the Peloponnese. 'What can they be chatting about?' wonders Agent Evangelos. 'Football, the high price of petrol, the new taxes, the weather?'

When he arrives on the neonatal floor, Agent Evangelos positions himself behind a pillar, well back, away from the lifts. Andromeda had texted him to let him know that her mother and her mother's partner were still in the room.

Agent Evangelos doesn't want to cross paths with his former wife, especially in such circumstances, and he's grateful to his daughter for the warning.

Through the thick window glass, Agent Evangelos can sense the noise of the city; he can't hear anything, but he can feel the sound waves coming from Kifisias Avenue; when he looks he can see the concrete landscape vibrate, and with every car that crosses the bridges he can feel the impact of the joints. His gaze is arrested by some big shopping centres, steel and glass giants capped with gigantic signs with pictures of Babis Vovos, the insatiable property developer.

The huge sign of Carrefour, the French supermarket chain, will soon be gone. The French are clearing out: Greece hasn't turned out well for them – unmanageable, and the turnover was insufficient; the colony has proved a disappointment. Agent Evangelos met them one 14 July, executives loosening their ties beside the swimming pool at the Hilton. The new ambassador, a graduate of the elite National School of Administration in Paris, had just taken up his post. The sun was beating down, and vintage wines sat in buckets of melting ice. The reception was attended by diplomats and investors, representatives of the Franco-Hellenic Chamber of Commerce, all upper-crust, bankers large and small, a consul, military men from the Saint-Cyr military academy on one hand and from the Marine Regiment on the other, the Crédit Agricole as a bridgehead, bosses and underbosses. Danone was there, as were L'Oréal and Citroën, upper management sweating in the boiling heat of the brilliant reflection off the hotel as the inferno of the setting sun lingered on its western facade: the French roasting in their suits, BNP Paribas and two young know-alls from the Société Générale trying to outdo one another in witty remarks about their new Greek colleagues: "Don't even know the basics, do bugger all, drink coffee all day long, spending an hour over a Nescafé, you can't imagine; accounting methods out of the ark and a completely clueless HR department. But they're nice, no, really nice people, and the girls all speak French."

Behind the residential high-rises of Maroussi, Kifisias Avenue slips into the abyss of the motorway interchange. Soon, Giorgos will be paying the toll and they'll be on their way to the airport – twenty minutes; the control tower is already in view, solitary, looking from a distance like a water tower lost on the Plain of Markopoulos.

An officer is to meet him at Alexandroupolis Airport. This evening Agent Evangelos will be in Thrace, and he expects his colleague will drive him directly to the morgue.

"What's the little one like?"

To the left, beyond a little house with a patch of colourless sky falling vertically on its whitewashed roof, it is almost midday on the high tops of Filothei's trees, an intimation of the washed-out shade surrounding the residences with their perpetually lowered blinds – the kind that are always out of sight, both from here and below, for any view of them is blocked by walls whose height is increased by masses of blossom: hidden, not allowing the slightest glimpse through the complicated tracery of the gates closing their impressive entrances.

A few poplars rise above the ragged fringe of a pine grove which, farther on, traces the course of a little river, its existence unsuspected by the last show-business personalities living there, those who haven't yet moved into their new quarters on the heights of Ekali.

Agent Evangelos remembers coming as a child to play in Filothei when his parents brought his sister and him to visit an aged uncle of his father's, a retired judge. At the time there were hedges growing, and the walls hadn't been made intruder-proof; cascades of bougainvillea marked the approximate location of the frontier between the properties and the shady streets where there was not yet any CCTV glass eye to spy on the grey, intermittent comings and goings inscribed on the digital void of hours and minutes.

But the last time that Agent Evangelos came to Filothei, it hadn't been to get an orangeade from the stand at the street corner. It must have been in springtime, for the laurels along Kifisias Avenue were in bloom, it was very humid, and the leather seats of the car smelled of the warm errands of summers past.

The driver never spoke.

Agent Evangelos barely knew the driver, unlike Giorgos, a colleague with whom he felt entirely at ease, like today when they chatted as they drove. As they passed the American College, shortly after the turning to Psychiko, Agent Evangelos had turned towards the man to encourage him to strike up a conversation. But the man didn't respond; he was driving, and that was it, he wasn't a talker, but he could have tried to make a little small talk all the same: the weather, hot for the season, the strange humidity in the air, you'd have thought it was summer, but no, the guy headed straight for Filothei, a strange location for a meeting. They hadn't told him the address; the directorate had simply specified that a driver would pick him up in front of his office at the end of the day.

Agent Evangelos had grasped that he wasn't being chauffeur-driven that day. He was simply being brought somewhere for a discussion that was still a mystery to him. The car seats gave off a strong odour; they smelled of stress, like when you have to act quickly, when time is short, and when a heatwave over Athens makes it a trial to move about because of the excessive heat inside the car, your shirt sticking to your skin and you feeling the need for a cigarette again. The entire neighbourhood around the Polytechnic was cordoned off, he had never seen so many people in the street, in *episodia*, the destructive aftermath of demonstrations. How many? At least 5,000, heading up Stadiou Street from Omonoia Square.

The driver was distant and no mistake, not wanting any contact, not the chatty type, no possibility of an exchange, strictly under orders: Don't start a conversation, just drive him to 21 Andrea Metaxa Street in Filothei; stop in front of the entrance, the camera will recognize you, the gates will open, drive in, drop him off, and go.

Agent Evangelos well remembers the two gates opening on a little driveway, barely fifty metres long, with the house already in sight. The shutters were closed; dry leaves lay on the terrace, and likely on the balconies as well.

Agent Evangelos doesn't want to think back on the subsequent conversation in the sitting room of that house. His immediate superior was there. He didn't introduce the others: plain-clothes officers and higher-ups, top brass, something like that, his superiors, but no one he knew.

He'd rather forget about it, but this morning's meeting about the severed head in the Evros region has revived the memory of the whole episode, when he was given to understand that his investigation was being terminated, that he shouldn't try to be overzealous.

Yes, just like earlier today when his boss had told him, "Don't be overzealous. Above all, do everything you can to prevent this business of the head from getting out. Your mission in Thrace is to hush up the matter, do you understand? The way to handle it is to let people believe it's a migrant, you see – the victim of some accident, or settling of scores, whatever! But you'll think of something, I've every confidence in you."

Just like that day in that house in Filothei, when he'd been told: "We don't give a damn if Barbaros has connections with the Germans." "We couldn't care less if he's still a member of the KKE." "We don't care if he greases the palms of politicians on both the right and the left."

Agent Evangelos, who had believed he was doing the right thing, had learned that Barbaros, a former communist who had made his fortune selling electronic equipment and mobile phones, was now a major shareholder in several large daily newspapers, a board member of a private television channel and the owner of a big multimedia store in central Athens…

"And then there was that business about East Germany. Yes, his father, Barbaros's father was —"

"We don't give a damn, Agent Evangelos!"

Agent Evangelos had learned that Barbaros's father had been the personal physician of Erich Honecker, the leader of the German Democratic Republic from 1976 to 1989. That explained his German connections.

"And you don't find it extraordinary that these days the son of the East German president's personal physician is pushing for the purchase of arms from Germany? A former communist activist, now a businessman and press baron, Mr Barbaros?"

"Listen, Agent Evangelos, we're not unaware of those facts, but —"

"Objection: Barbaros contributed generously to the Right, who were in power during the electoral campaigns of the 2000s. In exchange, New Democracy promised this billionaire, even though he was still a member of the KKE, that it wouldn't break the armaments contracts between Greece and Germany. This influential individual has at least one good reason to cultivate the links between his country and Berlin: he manufactures the battery system that fuels the German-made torpedoes with which the Greek navy's submarines are equipped."

When he shared the results of his inquiry with the directorate, Agent Evangelos never imagined that it would be brought to an abrupt end, accompanied by a private lecture on the new strategic direction of the Greek armed forces and a "Case closed! It's the defence of Greek territorial waters in the Aegean that's at stake!"

That day, Agent Evangelos was about to reply when he was cut short by a wink from his immediate superior, who told him it was time to move to the small drawing room, where an Eastern-style buffet awaited the guests. Among them, Evangelos recognized Barbaros, although he was familiar with only a single public photograph of the man. All smiles, the vendor of submarine batteries handed him a glass of wine.

"Yes, but wasn't it precisely the opposition that pushed for this inquiry into the alleged bribes?" Agent Evangelos had just had time to ask, staring at Barbaros, who was gesturing to him to approach.

"True, but so what?" his boss had asked later, after the reception, when they were alone again, sitting in the car. "Always the same tiresome questions!"

"I don't understand it. PASOK, the opposition at the time, is in power now, and you're asking me to drop the case?"

"Oh, you're like a dog with a bone. You're being told to drop the case, that's all there is to it."

"By whom?"

"Agent Evangelos, you're getting old."

"You're not going to tell me that PASOK has benefited from his generosity as well?"

"Who do you mean?"

"Don't act stupid with me, please. I'm talking about that shit Barbaros."

"Well, then, you shouldn't have accepted his glass of wine!"

"Who brought me here this evening? It was a trap, you bastard!"

"Agent Evangelos, calm down! Let me ask you a simple question: who's in charge of Greece today?"

"PASOK."

Night was approaching, and the remainder of the conversation remains inaudible in his memory. But then, suddenly, it is still daytime, and Evangelos hears a baby crying. He hasn't left his corner in front of the window at the end of the corridor in the maternity clinic. Why does he always have to look so questioningly at Athens? Filothei, Maroussi, and it's already the foothills of Mount Pentelikon, Vrilissia and Melissia. At the end of the day, the new terminology imposed by the technocrats is perfectly adapted to this tormented urban geography: now we have "regional units" instead of "nomarchies".

The baby is bawling, a baby, his granddaughter, born on 22 December 2010, in Maroussi, in the regional unit of Athens North. She has entered the world exactly a year to the day since the Greek state's credit rating was lowered from A1 to A2 by Moody's because of the country's deteriorating financial situation.

'What does my granddaughter look like? What does she look like?'

This morning, in the head office of Directorate C of the National Intelligence Service, he was given clear instructions: to identify the dead man as quickly as possible and do everything possible to avoid the matter becoming public. For the government, this incident had come at the worst possible time. Just a week ago the Minister for Public Safety had announced that a "wall" (actually a barbed-wire fence) was to be built along twelve and a half kilometres of the land border with Turkey. This was a message addressed loud and clear to the European governments, for the project possessed both practical and symbolic value, being intended simultaneously to discourage illegal migration and to send the message that Greece could not be entered at will. Athens, stung to the quick by the criticism from Paris and Berlin, who constantly blamed it for allowing too many illegals into the Schengen Area, wanted to demonstrate that its frontiers were not porous. The wall would show that. But Greece was asking Brussels for euros to finance its construction.

"Excuse me?"

Evangelos jumps. The baby, and now the voice of a woman in a white coat, smiling at him.

"You are Mrs Tsimias's father?"

"Yes, that's me."

"Your daughter told me I'd find you in the corridor. You can go in to her now, in room 306."

Evangelos consults his smartphone: two unread text messages and three unanswered phone calls, all from his daughter. Andromeda must have thought he'd left. What was he thinking, standing there at that window? That the defence budget hadn't been cut by a single cent, that a submarine torpedo is still called a submarine torpedo, yet the division of Athens into administrative regions suffered an onslaught of petty cuts, forcing him to change the very way he thinks about the city of his birth? 'Regional units my foot.' Evangelos finds it hard to understand these economic measures, which he considers useless. Merging the Athenian municipalities won't save the state a cent. On the other hand, cutting the armed forces budget by a factor of two or three would have allowed a substantial reduction in the debt.

The door to room 306 is open. Agent Evangelos takes a few steps into the room and then stops, disconcerted.

"Come in, Dad!"

He sees her, he sees them, he sees the little one. He still doesn't budge, but for the first time in months Agent Evangelos smiles.

Antonis Antoniadis knows that the human fingernail grows continuously at the rate of a tenth of a millimetre a day. That means it takes six months for a fingernail to grow back completely. Twelve months for a toenail. But, contrary to common belief, the nails don't continue to grow after death. Like any cell in the human body, the nail matrix must be irrigated by blood to produce keratin. So, when he bites his nails, Antonis Antoniadis is definitely alive; his nails are growing back. And he can bite them again, for in any case they'll grow again. But this cycle is the result of a partial death: keratin is a protein produced by certain skin cells. These cells continue to store keratin for as long as they produce it, but when they are completely full of it they die and become hard. Each dead cell then becomes a tiny piece of nail, pushed out by new keratin-producing cells. This is why the nail grows a little every day, and it is also why Antonis Antoniadis consumes his with a regularity that demonstrates his principal quality: he is a methodical person.

Indeed, the man responsible for the morgue in the University General Hospital of Alexandroupolis has an orderly mind, and Evangelos doesn't doubt it for a moment.

"No. 2666rb, you see, is in the same condition as when it was found." Adroitly, Antonis Antoniadis removes a human head from a transparent plastic bag and holds it up in front of Agent Evangelos, whose gaze follows it unflinchingly.

"Of course, it didn't have as much beard. Contrary to the widespread notion, hair doesn't continue to grow after death. What happens is that the skin becomes dehydrated, leading it to contract…"

Evangelos looks at Antoniadis's fist gripping the hair of number… of number… what was it again?

"2666rb. Yes, it's not easy to remember, but it's our numbering system, you understand."

The clenched fist of the forensic pathologist, a very slender young man in his thirties, whose fingers are white in the bright light from the morgue's ceiling fixtures; his fingernails are bitten to the point of bleeding. Disgusting!

"A clue already," mutters Evangelos. "The guy's a worrier, beneath his nonchalant air."

"A clue?"

"No, no, just talking to myself."

"But no, I heard you clearly, a clue, you said, whereas I only work on facts, sir. The head has told us what it has to say, and I've taken note of everything."

Whose head? It has no name. A male head. A man's head, no doubt about it, you can tell from the shape of the cranium. And in any case there's no need for a more detailed examination of this one, which is well preserved, not like some that are swollen and have turned black.

"You sound as if you had some in your refrigerated containers every day," Evangelos tosses out. "Do you collect them?"

"We get several a week going through here," sighs Antonis Antoniadis. "Not pretty ones either, believe me, drowning victims by the sackful, five of them a month."

Evangelos knows what the pathologist is talking about. Never fewer than three hundred people enter Greek territory illegally through the Evros region every day: Afghans, Pakistanis, Tunisians, Moroccans, Algerians, Somalis, Bangladeshis – more than seventy-six nationalities have been listed by the Orestiada police. And out of that number some never reach the opposite riverbank, the Greek side, the European side, the Schengen Zone.

"Right," says Evangelos. "Then tell me what else this head has told you."

Suddenly, Evangelos feels dizzy. He sees Samothrace again through the aeroplane window, the island directly below. 'What did I eat recently, on the plane?' he asks himself. 'A tuna sandwich. It's suddenly sitting heavy on my stomach.'

He says quietly, in a blank voice, "Leave that, Antonis, put it on the table."

"When I said I saw dozens going through here, I was talking about heads with an appendage – with a body attached. But some migrants who have drowned arrive completely naked, especially ones that have been in the water for a long time, and when they do still have clothes it's rare to find an identity card in their pockets."

"Obviously."

"Obviously."

"And not in this specific case," says Evangelos, suppressing an urge to vomit.

"Here, certainly, we don't have much. Apart from the head. Apart from this head which, as I told you, has told us all it has to say."

Evangelos is wondering where the toilet is. The doctor is going on and on, now explaining to him that he should forget about the entire head and just look at the face: "But by the looks of you, you won't have time, you're not looking so great yourself, ha ha! No, forgive me, your face, it's turned quite ashen, I mean, yes, of course, the toilet, don't worry about it, habit, I understand, me, you know, in my case familiarity breeds contempt."

'I caved in. I couldn't take it any longer. That head…'

He couldn't take it, Agent Evangelos. Dammit, a head like that sitting on the table, seeming to squint up at him. He just had time to listen to the forensic report: not very much to go on, apart from certain details that seem to prove they are not dealing with a migrant.

'I feel dead tired,' Agent Evangelos tells himself. 'What the hell is Stefanos up to? I can't take another hour in this stench.'

"Antonis? There was something else I wanted to ask you," says Evangelos, returning to the room. "What's that smell, what is it? It reminds me of something. But I just can't remember. What's that smell, dammit!"

"Try to think what it reminds you of," answers the pathologist. "Search deep down within yourself; put it into words; but it's best of all to not think about it."

Evangelos shrugs. He remembers there are still photos to be taken, from every angle, for his superiors, and then maybe for Interpol, even if his bosses had told him that he'd have to wait before broadcasting to the world about this head, this head that had committed the faux pas of falling to the ground inside a prohibited military zone. Its discovery couldn't fail to add to the salvos of criticism aimed at Athens. If it admitted that the head belonged to a migrant, the Greek police would surely be accused yet again of being incapable of ensuring the security of the border with Turkey. Greece is already being singled out for letting illegals into the Schengen Area. And if on top of that they arrive in pieces...

Stop thinking about it! Agent Evangelos takes his leave of the pathologist and goes outside to wait for his colleague from the local unit of Section C of the National Intelligence Service. Something moving over there on the plain – a reflection off a car window, a brief flare, the glint of a fisherman's lure: no, merely the sun filling the empty space behind the hospital, on the side where the wards are, at the time of day when patients ask their visitors to raise the blind to allow them to admire the sunset.

Still no sign of Stefanos. The evening is warm for the time of year. Under the awning over the emergency department entrance insects gyrate in the headlight beams of a colourless car. Its engine is turned off. All its doors are open. There is no one to be seen.

Agent Evangelos sniffs the sleeve of his jacket to make sure he hasn't brought the smell of the morgue with him. Outside, the air has no smell, nothing to eclipse the stench from inside. There is no breeze, and the sea is too far away to create an illusion. Beyond open country lorries glide along the southbound lanes of the Egnatia Odos, a silent film of lit-up tarpaulins. In the truckers' weary vision, the crossing over the Evros is near; soon the motorway will be reduced to a single lane as the trailers clatter across the bridge that intersects the dark line of the river, then they will be in Turkey with the border post at Ipsala leaping into rear-view mirrors that reflect the drivers' faces, grey in the intense light.

Agent Evangelos would like to have a chair to sit on. This is the second time today he has been driven to a hospital. The Alexandroupolis hospital is nothing like the Mitera Clinic, the doll's house surrounded by marble works where his granddaughter came into the world.

The baby was in a tiny, entirely personal cot, to which a blue and white label was attached by a bow adorned with a rabbit and a tiny bell. It displayed a number and a name: his daughter's married name. Until the little one is baptized they'll call her *Beba*.

'So, what's become of that wanker Stefanos?'

Agent Evangelos had never met Stefanos before today. He only knows the guy is terrified at the thought he might put a foot wrong – in other words, open his mouth and say too much about the head, allowing the media to get wind of the matter, with the dreaded consequence that a horde of media people would arrive and start nosing around the Evros delta.

"That's all we need," Stefanos had said when he met Evangelos at the airport.

'Stefanos, about my age,' he thinks, 'maybe a little younger; is it possible I'm sixty already? Do I see myself as a grandfather? I'm a *papous*!'

Since three o'clock this morning Agent Evangelos has been a grandfather, a *papous*.

'What did Stefanos say?' He tries to remember. '"There are enough nosey parkers around already, what with Frontex, those police officers from all over Europe, all with their little practices, the migrants, the traffickers, the prostitutes, the pimps, the dealers. All that's missing is the Athens media, the Athens newspapers." He gave me an odd look as he said "Athens".'

Two hospitals in one day. Agent Evangelos consults his mobile for the time; Stefanos is late. Two hospitals, but this one is on a completely different scale from the Mitera Clinic: it's a mega-complex, six kilometres west of Alexandroupolis, the biggest hospital in Greece, a sink-hole for European money. Solid, heavy, modern, Herakles cement, solid construction, concrete, glass, more than six hundred rooms, dozens of labs, over-budget before it was completed.

Agent Evangelos goes across to the car with the open doors. He hadn't noticed the family that had emerged from it a moment earlier go past. The daughter shouted something, and now the son is running to call someone, there's no one in the emergency department. Agent Evangelos remembers another scene: the father-in-law already on a stretcher, far along the corridors; the LED lamps in his face; the surgeon's eyes, stainless steel, all that white; must give the doctor the envelope with the money; the chest pains began in the back bedroom, the evening before, under the naked bulb, that stitch in his left side, the shadows on the northern wall where there are traces of moisture, and now so much light, the surgeon's eyes, the envelope before the operation or after?

All the car's doors are open, and the headlights are on. Agent Evangelos didn't see it arrive. Nor did he see them arrive, the family. It's only now he's looking at the dust-covered car as the insects whirl frantically in the headlight beams.

And now too, far inside the hospital, the father-in-law stretched out, his daughter holding his hand: decortication of both layers of the pericardium. The surgeon washes his hands, the suppliers paid cash for all the instruments, the ten-millilitre syringes have run out, we'll just have to put the right dose in the twenty-millilitre ones; the supply of tampons is declining visibly, getting surgical gloves, they were bought on credit in a city-centre pharmacy; he'd get them, for he's famous, the surgeon, he mustn't leave, the region needs him. The generic disinfectants will soon run out; a week from now the cardiology ward will have to shut down if the hospital doesn't pay the eight hundred thousand euros it owes – overall billing, delays everywhere.

'The envelope before the operation or after?' wonders the father-in-law.

Night is falling; the foul atmosphere of the morgue is dispersed in the evening air. Agent Evangelos is standing in front of the car, looking at the yellow dust that clings to the dull reflections in its paintwork. His gaze is lost in the light from the emergency department, caught in a thick ochre layer, the rich soil of the hinterland. Evangelos breathes in every speck of it, sniffing the scales the moths have shed on the windscreen. A familiar odour reaches him: the sweat of all those journeys, the dark stains on the rear seat, and then the smell of petrol, hanging, sweet and sour, all the odours of the day evaporating from the car's interior, and a kind of desire to believe in life again.

If he'd been in Athens Evangelos would have gone for a drink in the Batman.

The street was like a wave billowing into the city. Evangelos in front of the entrance to the bar, yesterday evening.

A vibration in his jacket pocket. It's Stefanos: *I'm on my way, sorry about the delay, the debriefing with the Frontex people lasted longer than expected.*

He'll tell Stefanos what he saw: 'A face with its eyelids half closed, its mouth half closed, a man with his eyes half closed, a swarthy skin, colourless eyes, dark hair.'

Evangelos no longer knows what he was supposed to see about this head: 'Hell, I don't know, I didn't see anything, what was I supposed to look for? The colour of his skin?'

The skin was pale on the forehead; the cheeks seemed dirty, with blackish crusts under the chin. The dark hair, thick on top, seemed set. The temples were bare, the ears shiny.

The skin was dirty.

"Yes, with blood, with dirt, but there's still no sign of tissue decay; and anyway it's white, this guy didn't come from the other side," the pathologist had said.

"From the other side?"

"From across the Evros, across the river, the frontier. They all come from the other bank. And when they get here, if they've not deteriorated too much after spending a long time in the water, you just have to see what they look like to know they've crossed the Evros."

"His nose and cheekbones. It's true, you'd take him for a European," Evangelos had remarked.

"Caucasoid," rectified the pathologist, rearranging No. 2666rb's hair.

"The *barbounia* are locally caught." Stefanos thought it useful to point that out. Red mullet don't come from Thailand.

Agent Evangelos looks up from his plate: "And the toothpicks?"

"What about the toothpicks? There's a container-full, there, beside the salt."

"Where do the toothpicks come from?"

"You're taking the mickey!" says Stefanos.

"Let me tell you," Evangelos goes on, "those toothpicks are from China and the wood was cut illegally in some part of Asia, in some forest that loses an area the size of a football pitch every day."

"Maybe so."

"No, there's no doubt about it. The same applies to the chairs."

"To the chairs? Really?"

"You'd think they were old-style taverna chairs, but actually they come from China. The Piraeus is Chinese too. So, you see, *barbounia* will always be able to swim in Greek waters —"

"Well, anyway, what about telling me how things went at the morgue?"

Agent Evangelos looks at Stefanos, he looks at this man his own age, an intelligence officer like himself; he sees him tearing off a corner of the tablecloth, a square of paper attached with clips, paper lined with plastic with a map of Samothrace printed on it in blue, and the name of the taverna entwined with a drawing of a caique framed by a fishing net. The sea is across the street. Over the water, a dark shape, a mountain: Samothrace.

An intelligence officer his own age, tearing the table-cloth, with a question on his lips like a morsel of fish.

"There wasn't anything of use at the morgue."

"Nothing at all? How can that be? You saw the goddamn head, all the same! What does it look like?"

"It doesn't look like anything, frankly. But the teeth were informative."

"The teeth?"

"First-class dental work: four amalgam fillings in the molars, and three composites of the latest type as well. He'd visited his hygienist very recently. And the patholo-gist even said he must have brushed his teeth shortly before he died, for he didn't find any remnants of food. If that's the case, he must have flossed after every meal."

"Well, that doesn't get us very far," sighed Stefanos, examining a toothpick as if it were a piece of evidence.

"You don't understand what it means? This head can't have come from a typical migrant of the kind that enter Greece every day through the Evros region."

"You're suggesting that the head came from a Westerner?"

"I didn't say that, and what's up with all you people and this so-called Western appearance? It just happens that we have a head that tells us it was someone with enough money to pay for the latest kind of dental care. So we can forget right away about the poor folk lining up to cross the river in the hope of finding an earthly paradise in Europe."

"Yes, but the migrants aren't all poor, you know. Apparently there are even teachers and doctors among them. The Frontex guys told me they'd picked up an Iraqi museum director."

"Stefanos, how many times in the day do you brush your teeth?"

"Morning and evening, why?"

"This evening, are you going to brush them?"

"You're taking the mickey again, is that it?"

"No, it was just to find out if you always go around with a tube of toothpaste in your pocket."

"I don't get it."

"What I'm saying is that anyone who has to pay people-smugglers to get him across the big river and into the Schengen Area most likely won't even have rinsed out his mouth for weeks. And if you went poking around his teeth you'd see some remains of the doner kebab he ate for his last meal in Istanbul before he found himself freezing his balls off in an inflatable boat on the banks of the Evros, waiting for some nice people-smuggler to pack him off to the opposite shore with a good kick on the backside."

Stefanos shrugs.

But there's still something else, thinks Agent Evangelos, taking a crumpled twenty-euro note from his pocket and throwing it onto the soiled tablecloth.

"There's another thing…"

Stefanos has stopped listening.

'Yes, another thing,' thinks Evangelos. 'It's the way the head was severed. The pathologist was positive. It wasn't a clean cut, yet it caused the victim's instantaneous death. The blade must have been very sharp, for no great strength had been required.'

"Stefanos, are you listening? Whoever did that didn't approach it like an execution. He didn't cut the head off cleanly."

"He. Or she."

"What are you suggesting?"

"What do we know? It could just as easily be a woman. These days…"

Agent Evangelos could have said, I think it's time for bed; you're tired, and so am I. But he says nothing, so naturally Stefanos doesn't answer, extricating a fragment of fish bone with a toothpick Made in China.

Episode II

That is where the head was found. It was there on the ground when it was discovered yesterday evening by the Finns from Frontex – in that precise spot, between the shed, which stands a little way back from the road, and the river. It was lying here at Lieutenant Anastasis's feet, face to the ground, on the dirt path, a little before the first thickets indicating the presence of marshland, a few metres from the line marking the start of the military zone.

'A shed, it's definitely called a shed in the report by the young Orestiada police officer,' Agent Evangelos repeats to himself, frowning. With a sudden movement, he turns up his jacket collar. It is almost midday and the sun still hasn't showed itself above the plain. The entire Evros region is afloat in a uniform mist, laden with evaporation from the marshes.

With Stefanos driving, it took over two hours. In Alexandroupolis, the dawn had been bright. Drinking an early coffee across from the station, where two Africans had just arrived on foot, exhausted by the night-long walk to the train that will take them to Athens if they can raise the twenty euros they need, a half-moon was still visible, suspended over Samothrace.

But as soon as they were on their way, after crossing the railway track on the outskirts of town and a long stretch across a barren plain, once the main road began to run along the Turkish border, heading due north, the pale substance of the day had dissolved into the mingled vapours from river and sky. 'And now you have to deal with a damp that seeps into your bones and strips you naked.'

Stefanos is jumping on the spot to warm up. In his black leather jacket, Lieutenant Anastasis ignores the cold. He doesn't look like a police officer, with his little beard and his thirty years. He smokes in silence, observing Agent Evangelos's reaction, for he already knows what the intelligence officer will say: "It was you who signed this report, wasn't it?"

A murmured "Yes."

Evangelos continues, "The river is there, behind those trees, five hundred metres away, isn't that so?"

Clearing his throat, the lieutenant agrees. "Yes, behind the trees."

"And according to you that's a shed?"

"That's what it looks like."

Agent Evangelos turns abruptly towards the young lieutenant and points at a little red sign, planted in the middle of the field.

"What does it say?"

"Military zone. Keep out."

"So you do know how to read!"

Stefanos, shocked, approaches and starts to say something. Agent Evangelos doesn't give him the chance, and addresses Lieutenant Anastasis again: "If you're able to read, tell me what's written on your damned shed? I know it's in Roman letters, but never mind, you're a police officer, you went to school, didn't you?"

The lieutenant looks straight at Agent Evangelos, whose expression, as anger sweeps over him, no longer betrays his fatigue of the past few days.

"I asked you a question! What's written up there in pink lettering?"

"Eros…"

"And it's even a Greek word! So what does it mean, can you tell me that?"

"Please, sir —"

"But for God's sake why didn't you mention the presence of a brothel in your report? Your damned shed is a knocking shop!"

"I didn't see why it was so important."

"Then either you're an idiot, or you're messing me about. A head is discovered fifty metres away from a brothel, and you take it on yourself to ignore that fact!"

"Easy, Evangelos!" says Stefanos. "You know as well as I do what goes on here every day. Lieutenant Anastasis sees dozens of illegals coming ashore morning and evening, the guys from Frontex tramping through his office, Germans, French, Romanians, all in uniform, asking him for reports, with the Estonian patrol coming into the police station to turn their guns in to the armoury before they go back to their hotel rooms. Every week he has to submit a report to the army. That's the reality we have to live with around here; people screwing in some goddamn shed in the countryside is irrelevant, we're at war here, Evangelos, it's an invasion! It's high time you people in Athens understood what it's like here on the Evros."

Evangelos shrugs. "Stefanos, your frustrations have nothing to do with me! And keep your comments about immigrants to yourself! Now, Lieutenant, tell me why you didn't mention the presence of this brothel."

The young man doesn't answer. The look in his eyes isn't typical of a policeman. That's not the kind of look the masked motorcycle police in Athens give people, thinks Evangelos, who hates the way they look at you these days, like under the Colonels. But in the lieutenant's case it's a different look in his dark eyes, something else, a quick glance that comes from somewhere deep down, a pair of eyes that go through you, a look not of fear, not of irony, not a challenging look, but one that turns you back on yourself; a reflection, that's what it is, a shared look, the same unbending recognition of the new order of power.

So Evangelos lets it drop; he understands why the young policeman didn't mention the brothel's presence. It was because he'd been given the order from higher up. It's obvious, for the lad is intelligent and no one could have missed that pink lettering: Eros, Eros on the Evros, a pink neon sign attached to the first storey of a large cube of concrete and brick with two blind windows facing the river and a terrace on the first floor but no fence, a large sliding door facing the road, an entrance on one side with a white aluminium door, and those four enticing letters on the roof, visible from far off – Eros – less than a kilometre from the frontier, creating the only coloured vapour in the dense mist rising from the marsh.

Welcome to Schengen! Bitch of a Europe, with her legs wide open at the water's edge, and the illegals, chilled to the bone, crawling on the riverbank, looking for a way through the thickets to firm land, a slope to climb, a dark expanse to cross. A field? Feet bogging down, the sharp points of the corn stalks. At last! A light, very close! Friend or enemy? Erotic massage, OWC, KWT, 69, toys, COF: go through customs here!

"Right, so let's go and see what we can find inside this building," says Stefanos, cutting across the open ground towards the brothel.

Agent Evangelos, barely able to contain his fury, follows at a distance, and the lieutenant falls into step. The exchange can continue. Something has passed between the two men: an identical feeling of impotence.

"I imagine you already questioned the girls?" asks Agent Evangelos.

"When I got here a military patrol was already on the spot. They were erecting lights around the crime scene and sealing it off. Naturally, I began by going to see if the girls had heard or seen anything, but everyone had left, and what struck me most was the chaos inside. There were broken glasses, bottles everywhere, sheets rolled up in a ball, overturned mattresses, ashtrays overflowing with butts. Anyway, you can imagine the scene. But then —"

"A brothel, then!" Stefanos breaks in.

"Go on, Lieutenant," prods Agent Evangelos. "You were going to say something…"

"But then what struck me was that they had left some of their stuff behind. Suitcases, two or three bags. I thought I should have carted it all away, but the captain told me it wouldn't be any use to us, and that I was on the wrong track."

A few questions from Agent Evangelos: "You think it was all that activity that made them clear out?" "What made you change your mind?" "Oh, really?" "It could also have been the Frontex control that upset everyone, couldn't it? I imagine all those guys in uniform mustn't be all that welcome to the pimps?" "What makes you say that, Lieutenant?" "Wasn't it you who put all that in that damn report, Lieutenant?"

Lieutenant Anastasis's answers:

"I don't know, anyway. It's not they who decide their movements. Initially I thought it was the pimps who had given the alert when they saw the army jeeps arriving." "It was the scene inside the brothel…" "You'll see for yourself, I sealed off the building, but everything is where it was, like on the evening when the head was found along the path."

Evangelos says, "The way you present the facts suggests this whole business has a certain logic: the frontier, a crime, splendid Schengen guards paid for by Brussels…"

The lieutenant doesn't answer. The two men are now standing in front of the building. From afar, Agent Evangelos hadn't noticed the little fence that runs three quarters of the way around the brothel, or the neglected garden in which a rust-eaten tractor has taken root. Two metres from the front of the building, protected by a wattle fence and a few chipboard planks, this partly covered space forms a kind of exterior passageway. It is actually the entrance, hidden in shadow. On the side next to the road is a gravelled area, also hidden from view behind some potted shrubs: parking for the customers. To the west of the building, a pile of coloured sheets is mouldering on the ground.

Stefanos suddenly bursts from the little alleyway, quite breathless. "Someone has broken the seals!" Pushing Stefanos out of the way, the lieutenant rushes into the brothel. Agent Evangelos, shaking his head, steps after them, cursing the thick mist that now extends well beyond the Evros delta.

In his career, and in his life as a man, Agent Evangelos thought he'd seen all there was to see about brothels: the sordid neoclassical houses in the Aigaleo district, the foul apartments on Filis Street, near Victoria Square, the "love hotels" near Syngrou Avenue, the *skyladika* nightclubs of his teenage years when Pamis would borrow his father's Triumph to take his pals for a spin on the road to the north. But no, he'd never seen anything like this: a vast room oozing humidity, a foul, musty smell, and mattresses laid directly on a linoleum-covered floor stained and pitted with black cigarette burns.

"I don't believe it! It's all been cleared away; there's nothing left!" Lieutenant Anastasis is devastated. Evangelos hears him repeating, "It's all been cleared away! They'd left everything behind, their stuff, their bags, their suitcases, everything!"

Evangelos jumps on him. "And you didn't think it best to take the whole lot with you that evening."

"As I told you, I got orders from above. I was told not to touch the brothel, it would be a waste of time, that's exactly what the captain said."

Stefanos informs Evangelos that he is to meet the lieutenant's superior officer that evening. "You can sort it out then! The captain couldn't be here today. He's across on the other side, in Turkey. He has a meeting with the chief of police in Edirne to discuss the illegals. They get on very well, apparently. They agree about everything, but they also have superior officers who block everything."

Evangelos looks at Stefanos and the lieutenant in turn. He can barely believe what he's hearing.

"Let me explain," insists Anastasis. "When I went in I discovered an incredible shambles. There were over-turned suitcases, undergarments everywhere, undergarments that had got singed on the electric radiators. The girls slept here, and entertained their clients upstairs. Though 'clients' isn't quite the word... When they came in they could pick a girl by pointing at her bed."

"It's a pigsty, this brothel," exclaims Agent Evangelos.

"Before the migrants came I had time to combat sex trafficking, it was my field, but no more. I've been working in Orestiada for seven years, and each year there are more and more illegals, so that's all you have time for now: you register them at the station, you pass on the paperwork to Frontex, and in the meantime pimps and traffickers of every kind have free rein. I'd say this isn't just any kind of brothel, as the girls who arrive for the first time in this pigsty have never done prostitution before; this is where they send the novices..."

"The clients aren't unaware of all that, I imagine?" asks Evangelos.

The lieutenant is doing his best. "You're suggesting that that's what they're looking for? The men who come here are participating in the…"

"In the what, Lieutenant?"

"They participate in breaking in the girls. Here, anything goes. The girls who refuse get beaten, raped…"

"And not just by the pimps?"

"Exactly. But as I was saying, when I saw what I'd found here I was thinking about hauling it all away. It was a gift! There were the girls' bags, with telephone numbers, the addresses of hotels for the rest of their trip through Greece – but what do you know, I was instructed to concentrate on the head, and I barely had time to give the order to lock up the brothel and leave everything inside."

"Now where has Agent Stefanos gone?" Evangelos sees him coming down the metal spiral staircase leading upstairs.

"Look what I found!" he says. "It's really bizarre!" Stefanos is holding a bunch of wreaths woven from leaves.

"But they're… what's it called?"

"Ivy. They're ivy wreaths," the lieutenant explains, "and I've a bit of a theory about that; in fact, it's the only thing they've left here, the shits, they've done a proper job."

Too many questions are jostling inside Agent Evangelos's head. "You can tell me later about the ivy wreaths," he says. "As for the rest, do you think it was the pimps who came back for the stuff?"

"It's possible, but they're not the only ones who might want to eliminate every trace of the girls' presence here."

"Tell me frankly," sighs Agent Evangelos. "Have you finished playing your guessing game with me, Lieutenant?"

The lieutenant is about to answer, but he catches a glance from Agent Stefanos, who has a bizarre look as if he were trying to confirm something of which he too was already aware. Lieutenant Anastasis has never had any confidence in the intelligence service, and for him Agent Stefanos personifies it. The other one, Evangelos, is a different matter; he'll explain the situation to him later, about the ivy, and about the very special patrons of the Eros.

Agent Evangelos is about to turn back to the lieutenant, but a call comes on his mobile. It's Athens. He leaves the brothel; the others don't need to hear. Seen from outside, the building looks like a barge adrift in the fog. Agent Evangelos can no longer tell the direction of the river. As he finally replies to the directorate, a cold, clammy hand caresses his cheek: the corner of a sheet still hanging on a clothes line, a malodorous sail soaked by the all-encompassing mist.

From that side of the world comes distress. Every night it silently invades the course of the River Evros. Then, at dawn, it spreads its seeds across the fields, transparent in the light coming from the opposite bank. Towards midday, when the fog has finally lifted, it has reached the southern edge of Orestiada, where the town stops dead on the floodplain, at the precise boundary where graffiti-covered trains run, connecting with the Bulgarian town of Svilengrad and ignoring the older track that passes through Edirne, in Turkey.

Agent Evangelos was in front of the police station when he saw the column pass through the railway station and come up Vasileos Konstantinou Avenue, unseen by the accustomed gaze of Orestiada's inhabitants. Bearing the rumble of the Evros's invisible current, conveying the river's humours, reluctantly transporting a burden of silt, they come, the people from the high plateaus of the Pamirs, from the floodplains of the Ganges and the Brahmaputra, from the Rif, along a single route which nowadays disrupts the very precise plan of Orestiada, conceived in 1922 to welcome other refugees: the Greeks of Asia Minor.

Men, women, children, the elderly, they cross not only countries and borders. They also traverse bodies of water, never to return, driven westward by poverty, no matter its cause, provided it is left behind – all the world's misery that they hope to forget once they have crossed the river.

'That's not counting fresh layers of misfortune that will be added to the six hundred euros handed over to the people-smugglers,' reflects Agent Evangelos in the moment. 'Whatever is needed to emerge from this disaster that sullies the threshold of the European Union, where, in 2010 as in 1945, the Greeks rummage in dustbins searching for some scraps to eat tonight.'

The first migrants arrive in front of the police station. They are the youngest, barely more than children, aged fifteen or sixteen at most.

'You'd think they were painted black.' That is how Agent Evangelos sees them: painted black, with eyes like marbles. 'I know those eyes defined by fear, the fear that makes a man look away as you interrogate him in a windowless room, exposing the whites of his eyes as he avoids your gaze.'

Every year, tens of thousands of asylum seekers and people without any papers arrive in Greece. The great majority of the former, fleeing war-torn countries, are Afghans, Eritreans, Iraqis, Palestinians and Somalis. The land frontier between Greece and Turkey, which extends over some 150 kilometres in the north-east of the country, along the river Evros, has become the main crossing point for illegal immigrants to the European Union, accounting for almost half the illegal entries detected. To think that just two years ago, reflects Agent Evangelos, most immigrants crossed the Aegean in makeshift boats, to be cast up on the shores of the Dodecanese. The directorate has provided the figures. They are alarming. Between 2009 and 2010, the central Mediterranean route through Italy and the western Mediterranean route through southern Spain have seen a decline of between thirty and sixty per cent. At the same time, the route through Turkey and Greece has seen an increase of 345 per cent.

Agent Evangelos has been told that the number of crossings could amount to over a hundred and fifty thousand this year. In Greece, it has hitherto been the responsibility of the police to deal with asylum cases. Migrants are barely registered in a police station before they find themselves interned in detention centres, generally situated near the frontier. Access to application procedures for asylum remains restricted, even in Athens, where it is difficult even to report to an Aliens' Bureau. Asylum seekers kept in detention still risk being turned back. Agent Evangelos knows all too well that no improvements have been made to the reception facilities, which are practically non-existent. Greece has no triage system for new arrivals, nor a way to identify the most vulnerable cases. A good number of applicants must wait months before they can embark on the asylum process. During this time they are in danger of arrest, and risk expulsion. Here, everyone closes their eyes to the inadequate facilities and functioning of the reception centres, which don't yet meet international standards.

'How can we fulfil our commitments to reform the asylum process, now that the Greeks themselves are beginning to find it difficult to survive?' Evangelos often asks himself when he reflects on the desperate situation of those migrants who swell the ranks of the homeless in Athens. 'A fine excuse,' he sighs this morning, as he observes the young migrants stretched out at the entrance to the police offices. 'If only at least the youngest were granted preferential treatment or special protection because of their age. But no, Presidential Decree No. 114 simply failed to forbid the detention of immigrants who aren't yet of age.' Evangelos has heard of minors being listed as adults in the Hellinikon registration centre in Athens.

The lieutenant is keeping him waiting; he went to fetch something from his office. As for Stefanos, he is trying to set up another interview with the Finns of Frontex. The request has to go through the Frontex headquarters in Warsaw; it seems their cooperation isn't a given. But in any case, as Agent Evangelos very well knows, nothing is a given. He intends to take full advantage of his one-on-one interview with Lieutenant Anastasis to throw some light on this business of the brothel and the ivy wreaths, just not in the police station. They'll go off to the Goody's terrace on a corner of the town square, in front of the big glass building. They'll chat, as if casually. And afterwards there'll be the interview with the captain, Orestiada's senior police officer, who thought it preferable not to mention the brothel in the report.

Like frightened but hungry cats, the migrants approach the police-station entrance step by step. Encouraged by the daring of a few, an entire group finally sits down on the edge of the pavement. The duty orderly gestures to them to line up on a kind of covered terrace, divided from the street by a low wall. Agent Evangelos counts about ten of them, but families are already flocking up, a futile, disoriented crowd.

Now they must number around sixty. The people-smugglers have told them: Don't try to run away from the Greek police. On the contrary, go to the police station, it's easy. From the riverbank, head directly across the fields and you'll find the railway track; look for the railway station, then go up the street; it's on the right. They'll give you the white paper you need to stay in Greece.

In the migrants' vernacular, this document, printed on "white paper", conveys a false hope: it is a thirty-day authorization to remain on Greek soil, long enough to have fingerprints taken and undergo interrogation. Agent Evangelos knows the whole charade by heart: 'Under the Dublin II Regulation, all illegal immigrants picked up by the authorities are registered in the Eurodac database, located in Lyon. They are then given a document ordering them to leave the country within thirty days. Except that no one takes the trouble to inform would-be immigrants properly, so they continue to believe that the "white paper" is a residence permit allowing them a month to organize the next stage of their journey without any reason to fear the police. In fact, this document provides no protection whatsoever, for its sole purpose is to get them on file with the Greek police.'

Inside his little gatehouse, the duty orderly is sipping an iced Nescafé. He's waiting to be relieved and never as much as casts a glance at a woman who is collapsing, drunk with fatigue. Her three children look on; the smallest, barely three years old, begins to cry. At that moment, Lieutenant Anastasis emerges. In a fury, he shouts, "Hey! You, drinking your coffee! Don't you see they're dying of thirst? Go and fetch a few bags of bottled water from the news stand. Say it's for the police."

"I know, chief," says the orderly, "but Dimitris, at the news stand, gives me hell when I go to get water; he says he still hasn't been paid for all the times when —"

"It's an order! Go and fetch me water and some biscuits, right now, do you hear? Anyway, damn it, here, take these fifty euros."

Agent Evangelos has approached the woman lying on the ground. Some schoolchildren go along the pavement; they can't miss the scene, but they have witnessed so much misery every morning on their way to school that the word "pity" has been eliminated from their vocabulary, leaving only a sense of discomfort, a kind of impotence that makes them stare at the ground – themselves refugees, but evading their own anguish. Their children's minds are already filled with fathers losing their jobs, fuel bills their families can't pay, a grandmother's cancer that can't be treated for lack of health insurance. In any case the hospital even lacks the resources needed to provide care.

The lieutenant returns inside the police station and asks the receptionist for a blanket. He adds, "Bring some sugar too, and if you find a few leftover sandwiches, take them, pick up everything there is to eat!" As he passes Agent Evangelos he calls out, "If you'd be good enough to follow me to my office, I've no time left to go to the café to chat; it's too bad if we're overheard, but look, you can see there are just too many of them. The last time we saw a crowd like that arrive was in November."

And the border guards, where are they? Agent Evangelos is surprised, and wonders what they are doing. A military van with Hungarian plates and a Land Rover with Bulgarian plates are parked in front of the police station. But there's no sign of anyone from Frontex. "It's just that they're out on patrol, sir," says the young officer. "They're out on patrol, while we're in it up to our necks."

Agent Evangelos follows the lieutenant into a small, windowless room. The furniture consists of just two desks, three computers and dozens of coffee mugs brimming with cigarette butts. An icon of the Virgin squints bless-edly from the wall. There is also a calendar depicting local football teams, sponsored by a telephone company. It is open at June of the previous year.

"Forgive the mess," grumbles the lieutenant, "but we no longer have any budget for a cleaning woman in the evenings."

"I know how it is, Lieutenant, no need to explain."

"By the way," says the lieutenant, "have you heard the latest? The Troika is demanding new cuts, otherwise the aid tap will be turned off, and in addition we still don't know the date of the election, so the provisional govern-ment remains in place."

"Lieutenant, if it's to talk politics, let me invite you to my office in Athens."

The lieutenant sighs. "All right, but you have to under-stand that some days I don't know if I'm coming or going."

Agent Evangelos says nothing more. He is waiting for Lieutenant Anastasis to calm down. He watches him dig around in his packet of cigarettes and pick up the phone to order two coffees from the nearby restaurant.

Two men go along the corridor, heads down, hands behind their backs. They are handcuffed. A tall fellow with close-cropped fair hair pushes them ahead of him. He stops briefly in front of the office door. "Lieutenant, I'm bringing you two suspects. They were caught over by Nea Vyssa. Turkish peasants, I think."

"OK, OK, put them in a cell, we'll look into it this evening. If they're Turkish people-smugglers, the captain will have to be told right away. He's across in Edirne today."

The tall, blond man gives a curt nod of acknowledgement. 'All but clicking his heels,' thinks Agent Evangelos, who discovers that this is his first European border guard: Werner, the head of the Austrian patrol; an efficient fellow, unlike some of the others.

"Between the two of us, as I'm sure you've understood," confides the lieutenant, "I've no control over these Frontex people. They lord it over us, and their superiors accuse us of not doing our job properly. But what about them, I ask you? What do they do that we don't? All they do is register the incoming illegals to get them into their European database. And then what?"

Voices are heard in the corridor. More uniformed men go by; there comes a clunk of rifle butts, a clump of heavy boots on the stairs.

"Right, they're coming back, they're returning their guns to the armoury. Maybe we should go to Goody's to chat after all," sighs the lieutenant.

Evangelos looks at his watch. At the rate things are going, he tells himself, he might as well phone his daughter. And maybe take the first plane for Athens – especially since the instructions he was given by phone this morning were very clear: "Perhaps that head of yours didn't come from a migrant's body, Agent Evangelos. But if didn't, then it must have sat on a people-smuggler's shoulders, if you'll excuse that way of putting it. Let's be clear: this case absolutely must have something to do with illegals, or be some kind of settling of accounts. In any case, that's the direction to look in. As you well know, Agent Evangelos, all this validates our idea that erecting this barbed-wire wall is very urgent, with so many criminals crossing the border…"

The phone rings.

The call has come just as Lieutenant Anastasis is finally getting ready to say who took part in the orgies in the Eros brothel. That will have to wait, especially since the Frontex men, who are arriving by the dozen, are too numerous in the police station.

"It's for you, I think."

Agent Evangelos takes the phone. He recognizes the voice, it's Antoniadis, and he knows where the voice is coming from, because the smell from the morgue accompanies it. But it's not the smell of death. Agent Evangelos doesn't smell death with his nostrils; he sees it coming, he knows when it's on the prowl, but it's not because of its smell. When death is present, it doesn't smell, it no longer has a smell, and when the smell returns it's because death has already been there for a while.

When he found the British military attaché with three bullets in him, soaking in his blood behind the wheel of his car on the Kifisias Avenue bridge, just past the AB Vassilopoulos supermarket, Evangelos could see right away he was a goner. 'Why do I have to keep remembering it today, twelve years later?' Evangelos was on his motorbike that day, like the assassins. He wasn't wearing a helmet, and was just telling himself that Athens had a smell of its own: a mixture of eucalyptus essence, freshly baked bread, cigarette smoke and exhaust fumes.

Evangelos was on his motorbike, riding bareheaded – it was June, which explains how he could be on the spot only ten minutes after the shooting. He got there at the same time as the ambulance. When he found the Englishman slumped over the dashboard he immediately lost his taste for the city.

'When impressions are so strong,' he reflects, 'you don't feel anything, you lose your sense of smell, you just use your eyes to register the events.'

So too the smell from the morgue: 'What does that smell from the morgue remind me of? I don't know. But it wasn't fair. All those allegations, utterly false! Saying the Greeks had botched the inquiry into that assassination. I was involved, and I did everything possible to find the killers. *I* did, anyway. And I'm a Greek. And an intelligence agent, until further notice.'

"Hello, Agent Evangelos? Are you still there?"

"Yes, it's me, sorry, we've got a bad line. Do you have something new, Antonis?"

"You recognized my voice?"

"I can't forget it, nor that strange smell!"

"Oh, you're still on about that smell! You haven't worked it out yet, Agent Evangelos? Look within yourself."

"But why don't you tell me about that goddamn head? If you're calling me, maybe it has finally come up with something worth saying?"

"Yes, further analysis of the blood and the wound —"

"Spare me the details, would you?"

"Okay, the decapitation must have taken place less than an hour before the head was discovered. Scientifically, I'm sure of what I'm saying, and given the information from Anastasis's report I can deduce, as I said, that the Finns must have found the head right away, you understand?"

"Not a shadow of doubt, then?"

"No doubt whatsoever. And one more thing…"

"What?"

"The mufti called. He wanted to know if we could let him have the head when the inquiry is complete."

"Who? The mufti? Who is this mufti, pray?"

Lieutenant Anastasis, who has been listening closely to the conversation, frowns. "Could I speak to the doctor, Agent Evangelos?" he asks.

At first Evangelos pretends not to have heard. "But who is this guy, for God's sake?" he exclaims after a moment's silence.

"It's the mufti who buries the drowning victims; he digs graves for them in his village, Sidiro."

"Let me speak to Antonis!" insists the lieutenant, who has been following the conversation closely.

Surprised by his change of tone, Agent Evangelos hands him the phone.

"Antonis, it's me, Anastasis. How did the mufti find out about the head? What did he say to you?"

"As you know, the mufti is never very communicative. He just asked, 'You wouldn't have found a head, by any chance, because it would be good if we could bury his head too.'"

The lieutenant turns towards Agent Evangelos and exclaims, "If that's the case, we'll have the rest of the body! The Pomaks must have found it and buried it without saying anything. Let's pay the mufti a visit. I'll get a car."

"I won't budge an inch from here before you tell me who this mufti is, and how these Pomaks are mixed up in this business," insists Evangelos.

"I'll explain along the way; it's an hour's drive to Orestiada."

Agent Evangelos shrugs and follows the young officer, who strides through the police station, swearing as he goes. On the threshold, a new group of migrants has just arrived. Confused, they shiver in their damp clothes.

The lieutenant is driving in silence. He has put the blue light on top of the Jeep Cherokee and drives through the villages without slowing down. As for Agent Evangelos, he allows his thoughts to slip back to the desolate streets of Neos Kosmos and the pale glow of the Batman's neon sign; he is trying to imagine the wall, but he can only see impressions: images and faces of a fanciful Greece. Evangelos is wondering who that handsome young man can be, with his open shirt and flowing hair. A writer? A painter? His black-and-white photo was on the wall in the Batman. He always forgets to ask who he is. He knows the others: Kazantzidis, the singers, the ship owners, the actors, all those who have their pictures on the wall.

Agent Evangelos wants to phone his daughter. He'll suggest to her that they celebrate the little girl's birth at the Batman. He doesn't know why, but he likes the idea of going for a drink to celebrate the baby's arrival. Maybe the Batman isn't the right place for it, but it's where Agent Evangelos feels most at home just now. And since he's happy to be a grandfather it all makes sense.

'Why do we always have to compartmentalize everything?' he wonders. He has no trouble seeing himself with his daughter and the little girl and his friends from the bar, all assembled, with the old songs to celebrate the little girl's arrival into the world. He has no difficulty seeing that.

Now it occurs to Evangelos that he still hasn't seen the river: 'I haven't seen the wall yet either, and maybe it's not by chance.' Agent Evangelos tries to imagine what the wall can be like. 'One thing's for sure,' he reflects. 'It's that Brussels isn't going along, Germany especially, for Berlin doesn't want to give a cent to finance this barbed-wire fence to be unrolled along the only stretch of land frontier between Greece and Turkey, the sieve of the European Union, a yawning gap in the Schengen/Dublin agreement, twelve and a half kilometres of farmland south-west of Edirne, in an elbow of the Evros, before its long descent towards the sea. Brussels and Berlin aren't in favour of the Evros wall, but they might be prepared to subsidize the installation of surveillance cameras along the strategic frontier.'

But those are just words. Ever since they've been telling him about this river Agent Evangelos has seen nothing of it apart from a few clumps of trees drifting in the lingering mist, farther down.

In Evangelos's nebulous mind, confusion takes unexpected forms: ivy wreaths, a mufti's felt hat, mouldering sheets from a brothel. Suddenly, his head, feeling heavy after only twenty minutes on the road, is nodding on his chest. He is asleep.

The lieutenant explains to him about the mufti. "To start with, without saying anything to us, the Pomaks began to provide graves for the drowning victims pulled from the Evros. They couldn't accept the idea that Muslims might be buried without a proper ceremony. It was the mufti who had the idea of the cemetery. He had graves dug in the forest, just outside the village. He encountered a few problems when this was discovered. But, like the captain, we told ourselves it wasn't such a bad thing. Now, whenever they find a dead body, they phone us. We pick up the corpse and bring it to the morgue, Antonis examines it, and three months later, if it hasn't been claimed by a relative, it's handed over to the mufti. I'm talking about the deceased who don't have an identity card. And that means most of them!"

Agent Evangelos can't have been paying any attention to the landscape as he struggled against sleep, for he has caught only fleeting glimpses of vegetation, replaced here and there by monotonous rows of fruit trees.

"Here's what I wanted to tell you," says the lieutenant. "The real problem is Frontex. While it's true it's not easy to work with all those bastards in uniform, and they don't like us either, both of us know our job is pointless, as the migrants are still able to cross the frontier. We're hobbled by the same inability to act as the guys from

Frontex, except they're not in their own country. This Schengen frontier is absurd, but that's not what I want to talk about. The thing is that among the officers there are four guys who are real bastards."

With his eyes fixed on the road which is now rising onto a plateau, its relief dishevelled by stunted, wind-tossed scrub, the lieutenant goes on. "There are four officers who take part in the orgies in the Eros, and what's worse, they arrange a kind of scenario. They've reached an agreement with the pimp that they can use the girls any way they like. They require the girls to be nude, with ivy wreaths on their heads. They drug them before they abuse them, and the girls accept the drug to be able to tolerate the abuse, and if they don't agree – but they do – and if they don't, they're beaten, though it seems they're beaten to start with in any case. It's the Frontex guys who provide the dope."

Agent Evangelos has heard the lieutenant, who adds, "And it suits the pimps just fine, it makes their job easy. The girls end up in such a state that they can send them to work in the big cities, initially to Athens, then to Heraklion, and apparently to Patras in the past few months. I really don't know what kind of crap they give them, but it sends them into a trance; it seems they become as if hysterical, driven completely out of their minds. That's what those cretins seem to like – the Frontex guys, I mean."

Questions from Agent Evangelos:

"But how do you know all this?" "Does the whole Frontex personnel know about it?" "Why's that?" "But the higher-ups in Frontex, the other officers – the ones who don't take part in these goings-on – do they know anything about it?" "It remains to be seen, but listening to you it seems to me I'd better interview the Finnish patrol right away, for something tells me that they know more than what I was able to read in your report, don't you think?" "And the captain, your boss, what does he say about all this?"

Lieutenant Anastasis's answers:

"I sent one of my guys to observe one of the parties. I'd heard about these orgies a bit before that. People know about it, but nobody says anything. There are guys from round about who go along, just to watch." "No, but rumours are rife there. The problem is, those four bastards are officers. Their rank protects them, and it isn't in anybody's interest here for the whole thing to get out. Can you imagine the public reaction to a scandal like that? Frontex officers organizing orgies in brothels on the Schengen frontier! The whole Frontex agency would suffer. Actually, I think those bastards' colleagues have no idea about half of what goes on in the Eros. The captain says those guys can have as much fun as they want as long as he can keep control of all the operations to intercept migrants. In fact, he doesn't give a damn what goes on in the brothel."

'What's most infuriating,' thinks Agent Evangelos, 'is knowing that Frontex will do everything possible to protect its image, and therefore its employees.'

"Lieutenant, listen to me, this whole business stinks to high heaven, but I don't want to make a mistake. You're like me, you're looking for the truth, isn't that so?"

Suddenly, Lieutenant Anastasis brakes and pulls the Cherokee over to the side of the road with its engine still running.

"If you agree, let's try to find out the truth, even if we can't be sure that any kind of justice will be done."

If the preceding events represent the truth, it seems to be nothing extraordinary, because so far, even if the head found a body that could very well belong to it, there is nothing to indicate the identity of the dead man. In the basement of the hospital in Alexandroupolis, Antonis Antoniadis spends a sleepless night reassembling the various pieces of an unknown individual who had indeed been buried in a common grave in the village of Sidiro, thanks to the mufti's good offices.

The mufti was outside when Agent Evangelos and the lieutenant knocked on his door. He was stacking firewood on the flagstone floor of a house at the bottom of the village, too long under construction to ever be completed.

Bent over, his face hidden by a thick woollen hat, the mufti doesn't look up on hearing the two foreigners approach – for that is how he must consider his visitors. He carries on with his chore, even when his daughter approaches to whisper something in his ear. It is the girl who leads Agent Evangelos and Lieutenant Anastasis to her father, obeying the instructions shouted down a corridor by her mother, who is reluctant to come to the door. The youngster enjoys a definite advantage over her parents, as the lieutenant doesn't fail to point out. "At least she speaks excellent Greek."

"Why do you say that, Lieutenant?" asks Agent Evangelos.

"For the past twenty years, the young Pomaks have had to be educated in the national language. As I'm sure you know, the Greek government is looking for ways to wean the Pomaks away from Turkey. As a minority within a minority, they've long been under Turkish influence. During the past ten years, five schools that also admit the Pomak minority have opened in the region. No Turkish is taught in these establishments."

Agent Evangelos was on the point of replying that if this was accompanied by all the rights of citizens of the Hellenic Republic, he wouldn't have anything against such an advance in the educational system. But he has second thoughts, telling himself that this isn't the time to discuss the lot of minorities with Lieutenant Anastasis, especially since too many questions about the investigation remain unanswered, beginning with the ivy, which reminds him of something he can't quite put his finger on, not unlike that smell in the morgue.

When the mufti eventually looks up at Agent Evangelos, who has approached him, forcing him to interrupt his work, he doesn't utter a word. He just stands with his arms hanging, perfectly aware of the reason for this visit. He must be in his sixties, judging by his wrinkled brow and fine white moustache. Seeing that no question is forthcoming, he mumbles an *As-salaam 'alaikum* that evokes no response. Then, without further ado, he points first to his car, then to the jeep, signifying to follow him.

The sun is disappearing behind the hill overlooking the village as the mufti stops on the top of a little ridge. Beyond the red tiled roofs of the village, with its poor, white houses scattered across small hills of bare earth, the landscape resembles dense scrubland that has been chopped down to the soil along the length of a football pitch, but just ten metres wide. The cleared ground slopes, and rivulets of ochre soil that lead away from around fifty low hillocks form a delta of dried mud on the dead-end forest road where the vehicles have just stopped. What seems to be the cemetery is enclosed by a chain-link fence and its gate is secured by a padlock.

Still not uttering a word, the mufti takes out a bunch of keys and without further ado opens the gate of the resting place of the dead pulled from the Evros's troubled waters. A moist wind blows across the hilltop, raising little clouds of dust above the piles of earth, some of them long, others short, some narrow and others wide. Walking slowly, with bowed head, the mufti turns to the right and points to the most recent burial, at one end of a row of five graves.

He speaks for the first time, in an approximate Greek. "The man with no head is there, *inshallah*! Men from the village, they find him beside river, 21 December, morning, six o'clock. Like with all the Muslims that die crossing the Maritsa, they put his body in truck. It was dark night, all night, they look for head, *inshallah*! But scared, scared when see blue police lights."

"But can you be sure they're good Muslims?" asks Evangelos.

"We know many people who cross river come from Muslim lands. If not Muslims, we not know, but we take body anyway. We take all bodies."

Agent Evangelos also asks if anyone else was seen. The mufti seems to reflect for a moment, as if hesitant to say what he finally confides with a weary expression. "Them always hearing women crying, men laughing loud. But that evening, no noise, all quiet. Just saw police car, not a Greek one, and a minibus drive away. They tell me cars driving in dark, with no lights."

"Could you tell us more exactly where the body was found?" enquires Evangelos. The mufti informs him that the body lay at the river's edge and that it was naked; it didn't look like the other bodies the river gives up, it wasn't wet, it wasn't swollen and it was still warm, with much blood everywhere, *inshallah*!

Lieutenant Anastasis takes out his phone.

Later that evening, the mufti and the men from his village were present at what the annals of their community would record as sacrilege: twenty or so police from Alexandroupolis and Orestiada arrived, cordoned off the cemetery and installed floodlights that lit up the entire sky and the newly dug soil. When the body was exhumed from the latest of the river graves, *inshallah*! an expanse of starless night descended on the Pomak village. The dogs began to howl, the roosters to crow, and the sheep to bleat, *inshallah*!

Now it is late, though that doesn't mean much any more; events are following one another so fast on one another's heels, outstripping comprehension. Agent Evangelos leaves the office of Captain Giorgos Souflas, the very epitome of those obstructionists an intelligence agent inevitably encounters during his career. The mere contact of the captain's large hand, curiously dry and firm, makes Agent Evangelos recognize immediately that he is dealing with an impossibility. An enormous man, but at ease with his corpulence, jovial behind his moustache, authoritarian in his nonchalance, inspiring pity as he lights his tenth cigarette during an hour's conversation, almost choking as he draws on it with genuine pleasure; a large man smelling of eau de cologne, but above all formidably intelligent, the chief of police in Orestiada is on the verge of retirement. He has an unparalleled instinct for detecting the slightest threat to the established order – his order, in other words, starting with the setting of his chair, a notch lower than his superior officer's and a notch higher than his subordinates'. On the wall facing him are reproductions of icons of all those Orthodox saints who, each morning of every God-given day, do him the favour of reviving his clogged lungs by infusing them with the requisite quantity of auto-persuasion: the sense of being alive, fortunate and omnipotent, despite the presence of all those accursed people – not the migrants, towards whom the captain feels a kind of compassion inherited from the history of his own father, a refugee who arrived in Greece in 1922, not the migrants, especially since he knows they are just passing through, but those stupid big fellows from Frontex who strut through town in their national uniforms knowing all the while that the real boss around here is Captain Giorgos Souflas.

"Point taken," sighs Agent Evangelos, who despite all this has obtained what he wanted, namely a debriefing of the Finns and Souflas's collaboration in the inter-rogation of the four Frontex employees: Major Stefan Mankel, a German national, Captain Mikail Cerbonescu, a Romanian, Corporal Joseph Lumirascu, another Romanian, and Sergeant Sven Roboroski, a Pole.

Agent Evangelos had known how to get around the obstacle of Souflas. "If you don't collaborate with me, I'll say you're responsible for the inaccuracies in a report concerning the discovery of a severed head on the edge of a sensitive military zone."

"Are you crazy?" barks Souflas. "You don't know what you're doing; forget about the whole business of the brothel, and above all think twice about taking on Frontex single-handed. Are you looking for early retirement, Agent Evangelos?"

"If you weren't a little police captain in an eastern province with his fat arse sitting on what is now an ejector armchair," says Agent Evangelos, "I'd think you were trying to threaten me, but you don't scare me, and Frontex will answer for the abuses committed by its men, don't doubt it for a moment."

Agent Evangelos knows very well that he's bluffing. Frontex will transfer the culprits out, and do everything possible to stifle the affair. And already he can almost hear his superiors suggesting to him not to push his investigations too far. "There mustn't be the slightest risk of compromising the best interests of the country and endangering the security of its eastern border, which, as you very well know, Agent Evangelos, is under scrutiny from Brussels, and which we are attempting to strengthen at this very moment by erecting a wall to plug the gap."

Captain Souflas was saying the same thing in rather less diplomatic terms. And he is already recovering his smile as he says goodbye to Agent Evangelos, who has obtained more than he expected.

The night is going to be freezing cold, and as soon as he reaches the bottom of the town, along the railway line where the light from the neon signs becomes less intense and the yellow halo of the street lamps is turning grey, at the edge of the marshy plain which keeps Orestiada at a boggy distance from the Evros, from where the first migrants will soon be approaching under the indifferent lenses of the thermal cameras of the guardians of the Schengen Area who are posted on the heights above the river, as soon as he reaches the threshold of Europe Agent Evangelos will look up and see nothing overhead but an expanse that, star-strewn though it is, he finds empty and indecipherable.

The need to walk for a bit occurred to him quite naturally as he left the police station. His fatigue should have brought him back to his hotel, two blocks farther up on the left, but his feet led him towards the railway station. When he felt the ballast underfoot, all the repressed anger of the day drained away and, instead of crossing the track and entering the darkness, thus resisting its attraction, Agent Evangelos told himself he could follow the tracks for a while, and walk parallel to the river. In that way he wouldn't get lost, nor would he immediately become a pale silhouette on the screens in front of which the frontier guards are smoking silently inside their mobile surveillance post. And though he still wouldn't see the Evros he would be better able to imagine it, as if he were following its course between the rails.

But, as always, Agent Evangelos must struggle against unpleasant thoughts. The police captain's features don't disappear; they block his view, and there is no use telling himself that he is familiar with that kind of obstacle, since it always comes to him with the same appearance: the mocking eyes of that officer ordering recruits to beat up a student. It was in 1973, under the dictatorship, six years after the Colonels' coup; the recruits were refusing, protesting, saying no, but he just continued to smile; the obstacle remained, overweening in its confidence, making Evangelos betray his principles, for if he didn't toe the line he would be the one to suffer: "Go on, give him a few clouts, the goddamn student, don't you see he's shitting his jeans, with his long hair, and don't tell me, Evangelos, that you... he, he, Evangelos, hit him, hit him again, make him spill the beans, the filthy terrorist, don't be a softy, Evangelos!"

It's a clear night. Tomorrow the whole thing will be out in the open; it will be on the news, the internet will have the whole truth, lots of pictures on TV, eye-catching headlines on the front pages of the newspapers pinned up on the fronts of the news stands: "Shocking Murder on the Frontier"; "Frontier Guards Rape Women from Eastern Europe in a Brothel". Denials: protests from Berlin, Bucharest and Warsaw, disclaimers from Frontex.

The directorate knows about the raid on the Pomak village; soon the press will know as well, the releases are being copy-edited at this very moment; Agent Evangelos will certainly be in the hot seat. Why does this business have to come out now, just when the wall is about to be built? Of course, Greece isn't to blame, it's Frontex's fault, and Brussels is on tenterhooks – things could be worse, after all.

It is a clear, frosty night, but the stars provide no direction. Agent Evangelos has been walking for a good half hour, following the Evros along the railway line; he still hasn't seen the river. Tomorrow, if he has time, he'll ask the lieutenant to drive him there; time is short, they've got the rest of the body but they haven't made an identification yet, and the girls from the Eros have disappeared.

'Where did they go?' wonders Evangelos, hearing the frogs croaking in the ditch alongside the railway embankment that marks the edge of the plain, or maybe farther on in the marsh, and now the moon is rising on the gleaming metal of the rails, the frogs are croaking themselves hoarse, he can hear them, and it is in that moment, amid the nocturnal din, that he sees ivy wreaths on the brows of dancing women. Painted on the vases in black they are wearing ivy wreaths on their heads; he can see them in the display case in the Athens Archaeological Museum, black figures on a vase. It's the dance of the maenads: three pairs of them, and a couple of satyrs around a woman, all taking part in a lively, dancing chase.

They depict the dances that show how King Pentheus was torn apart by maenads, they describe the death of Orpheus: women with hair flying loose and ivy wreaths on their heads, dancing, carrying the *nebride*, brandishing the thyrsus as the laughing god looks on: there he is, enthroned in the centre of the scene, Dionysus offering them a cup; they cannot take the wine, it goes to their heads; they whirl and whirl, the wreaths fall forward over their burning faces; they chew a leaf, then another, the juices spurt in their mouths, bittersweet; six, seven, eleven bacchantes, forced to chew it all to the end, spitting nothing out, laughing! laughing! green tongues, vegetable breath, belches, laughter, laughter as the juice spreads through their veins. What has possessed them? They are drooling, contorted, eyes turned upward in the sockets, they are pale, enraged, hurling stones and then the thyrsi, aiming at the tree in which Pentheus is posted; they form a circle round its trunk; they make levers of oak branches to uproot the pine in which he is hiding, helpless, the overcurious man; they grasp the tree with many hands and rip it from the earth; Pentheus has fallen, and his mother Agave, sharing in the maenads' trance, his mother is the first to throw herself on him; she doesn't recognize him, he is guilty of having seen and learned. She is unable to feel as a mother should, and with Ino and Autonoë, her aunts, using the god's strength, she tears his shoulder away while Ino does likewise on the other side; the maenads finish rending apart the man who failed to understand the Dionysian power. Now Agave takes his head and sets it on the spike of her thyrsus.

With Pentheus torn in pieces and Orpheus beheaded, his inconsolable head continuing to weep for the woman whose very name enrages Bacchus's companions, the maenads become bacchantes; but it is Vergil reciting, Orpheus chanting eternally, a decapitation, a head falling, rolling in the river Evros, yet continuing to call the name of his Eurydice, rolling on the icy billows as it mourns the lost quintessence of its being to the river's mouth, where the sea jumbles the Thracian landscape.

Agent Evangelos allows his imagination free rein: the sound of the chants that precede the libations, then the dancing, the violent embraces, the cries, the howls, the ripping of cloth, the cracking of bones. Were it not for a sudden presence, he could have witnessed the entire scene: the hysterical girls writhing on the ground, on the floor of the Eros, their senses cruelly sharpened by the drug that delivered them abandoned to the excited men and their coarse laughter. But on the edge of the invisible river, Agent Evangelos discovers that he is no longer alone. Someone is coming towards him; he can hear the ballast crunch under a light tread. 'It must be a woman.' Evangelos is sure: 'It's a woman walking towards me.' She too is following the railway track, she too is walking in the open, close to the invisible meanders of the river. 'I'm not alone any longer; there are two of us following the Evros,' whispers Agent Evangelos. 'Does she even know that the river serves as a long wall? Does she sense its compact presence, the density of its current?'

Evangelos holds his breath. He keeps quite still, looking for the woman who will soon appear ahead, but the sound has stopped. Evangelos takes a few steps forward and stumbles against a doe. Taken by surprise, the animal looks at him for a fraction of a second, then bounds off into the thickets alongside the track, heading for the marsh.

With his heart thumping, Evangelos laughs to himself and resumes his nocturnal walk. Then his mobile vibrates. Evangelos answers. "What is it, Lieutenant?"

"Almost an hour ago a patrol found a woman wandering in the military zone along the frontier."

"A woman, alone?"

"Yes, and something tells me it's one of the girls from the Eros."

"Where is she?"

"In my office."

"I'm coming, I'm quite close."

Leaving the railway tracks and returning to the first houses in Orestiada, Evangelos overtakes a column of migrants advancing in single file that he fails to notice. Like them he is making for the most brightly lit street in the little border town, which leads from the railway station to the main square, passing the school and the police station.

At the entrance to the latter, twenty or so women and children are sleeping on the poorly lit terrace, in a row on the bare ground. A stray dog sniffs at the feet of a young boy whose running shoes are covered with mud. A putrid stench of wet earth and mould floats in the air.

"How many this evening?" asks Agent Evangelos.

"Twenty-six, all women and children," replies the orderly. "But more are coming."

Evangelos doesn't turn around. He enters the corridor, where he encounters a member of the Frontex police with the Danish national insignia on his shoulder. The door to Lieutenant Anastasis's office is open, and he spots the girl right away. His young colleague is in his chair, facing the young woman, and motions to him to enter.

"She's refusing to talk."

Evangelos takes a step forward and sees the girl shrink back on her chair and make as if to shield her face.

"She's scared," says the lieutenant, who looks worn out. "Yet I've been as gentle as a lamb with her."

Evangelos takes a chair and sits down beside the girl, who looks down at the floor.

"Don't be afraid, we're not going to hurt you."

Evangelos tries to meet the young woman's gaze. "I'm not going to hurt you, do you hear? Do you understand what I'm saying to you? You don't speak Greek, is that it? You're shivering. Here, take my jacket."

The girl doesn't reply; she sinks a little bit deeper into her chair. Evangelos looks at her: she is holding her head against her knees, he observes her delicate hands, resting on her skull, and her very fine blonde hair. Her false nails, painted a pale green, are broken, and her pale skin is covered with scratches. She doesn't answer.

Agent Evangelos turns towards the lieutenant, who passes him a cup and points to a thermos of coffee.

"Have some of this. Something tells me you need it."

"Thanks! Leave me alone with her for a moment. I'll sit in your chair."

The lieutenant shrugs and leaves the room.

Agent Evangelos goes over to the young woman and places the cup of coffee on the desk, within her reach. With slow, deliberate movements, he places his jacket on the shoulders of the girl, who sits up.

Only then does her face appear: a lovely face devastated by terror.

In the streets of Athens, late in the afternoon, printed in large black or red letters, swinging in front of the news stands from cords to which they are attached with clothes pegs, broadcast continuously on TV, mentioned every hour on the radio, and already the newly unemployed, the retired folk poking through rubbish bins, the laid-off dockers of Piraeus, the striking civil servants, the representatives of the electricity company expecting to be let go, and whose job it is to cut off the current to families who no longer pay their bills, the police in their masks, the anarchists in theirs, the shopkeepers who have lowered the blinds of their shops for the last time, the migrants who are learning Greek from the newspaper headlines, the pregnant women in public wards, the unpaid nurses, the young, underpaid interns in public hospitals concerned that the last available stocks of painkillers are dwindling fast, the heroes of the resistance to the Nazis begging for leftover scraps of chicken in the backyards of tavernas, the idle waiters and waitresses in cafés, the teachers who can no longer afford heating, the stay-at-home mothers who have maxed out their credit cards, the banker who is contemplating suicide, the young researchers working on contemporary poetry who no longer have the funds to travel to a university in Thessalonica, the schoolteachers who are asked to clean the school toilets themselves, the grandmother who no longer dares to leave home because of the addicts sleeping on the pavement, the kitchen staff in the Hotel Grande Bretagne who salvage leftovers for the old folks in their neighbourhood, the young couples six months behind with the rent, their landlords who no longer know how they can manage with all the tenants in arrears, the supermarket sales assistants who no longer have the means to pay for a tinting at the hairdresser's, the hairdresser who is closing up shop, the municipal employees who no longer collect the rubbish: all of them, if they are in Athens, now have something to talk about.

"Human Trafficking and Frontier Security".

"Sex Slaves to Frontex Officers".

"Evros: Scandal on the Schengen Frontier".

"A Brothel Controlled by Frontex Guards".

"European Agency Responsible for Outer Frontiers of Union Compromised in Sex Trafficking".

"The Sordid Patrols of the EU's Border Guards".

"Evros, Brothel of the European Union".

This morning on the phone, the directorate seemed pleased: "Good work, Agent Evangelos; the European Union is in a real pickle, and we're in a strong position to request funding for the construction of the wall. Governments are in chaos, the German embassy has created a crisis unit, they want to send their own investigators; it's sheer panic in the Frontex headquarters in Warsaw."

This affair couldn't have happened at a more opportune time for the Greek government. The directorate was jubilant: "Who, in Berlin, Brussels or Paris, can now accuse Greece of lacking vigilance on the Evros frontier?" Frontex, with its corps of European border guards, would now be the butt of all the criticism. In the circumstances, how could there be any opposition to funding the wall? To think that just a week earlier the European Commissioner responsible for security had said, "Walls or fences are short-term measures that don't allow us to tackle the question of clandestine immigration in a structural way." Now the proof is in: Frontex is doing a lousy job – maybe even worse than lousy. Now no one will dare to say that the Greek wall is too expensive. It will seem the only logical defence against unwanted migrants.

Requested to return to Athens the next day for a debriefing, Evangelos couldn't believe his ears. Back in his hotel room, he read the newspapers. He had had only two hours' sleep the previous night, and felt like throwing up; he was swallowing pills and could still hear the directorate on the phone – the battery of his mobile was almost dead, since he'd forgotten to recharge it, so he stayed close to the outlet where his phone was plugged in, asking his directorate for an extra week in Orestiada: "Just a week, that's all, the investigation isn't finished, it's just beginning; we haven't identified the dead man yet, and a police patrol has found one of the girls from the brothel wandering on her own at night in the restricted zone, completely lost. She must surely have things to say; it may well be that she had something to do with the murder."

The directorate got the message: "Yes, the girl; good job, Agent Evangelos. The Orestiada police have informed us; they'll take her statement. She'll have to make a clean breast of everything: the frontier guards, the abuse, the rapes; it's those bastards who are responsible. We have the guilty parties: they're sitting ducks, identified by the girl. After that, she'll be sent back to her own country. You'll be able to get her to talk, Agent Evangelos, but concentrate on the human trafficking, stress the fact that Frontex is involved: that's all we need to make the case for the wall."

The directorate insisted that the matter of the decapitation could now be handled perfectly well by the local police, since it was likely some underworld settling of scores unconnected with the scandal of the European frontier guards, the proof being that not a single evening newspaper was going to mention it: "Yes, yes, the media are on to it, but there's still not a word about the head, no, as far as the head goes they're still in the dark, and you deserve our thanks for that, Agent Evangelos, yes indeed, congratulations on your discretion; yes, that's right, no one has found out about the head. You've done a good job!"

"Yes, but the girl was scared stiff," Evangelos replied. "She hasn't opened her mouth. I tried to get her to talk yesterday evening; she probably knows something, I even think she may be involved. We still have to analyse her clothing, to see if there are traces of blood. I'm not going to drop the case just like that, and the Frontex guys aren't even behind bars, which is incredible in itself. And why has all that been released to the media so soon, for that matter?"

"Don't be overzealous, Agent Evangelos. This murder is an unnecessary complication. For Athens, what counts is the scandal around Frontex. The more the frontier guards are implicated in sex trafficking, the more our government can demand that Brussels come up with the funding required to build the wall. Surely that must be clear enough, isn't it?"

It was a short while ago that Agent Evangelos drew back the curtains and looked outside; he'd just finished speaking to his directorate, there was pale sunlight and a kind of smoke over the dew-covered roofs, and now, at almost five in the afternoon, he closes the door of Lieutenant Anastasis's windowless office.

"Do you realize, Lieutenant?"

"Just let it drop!" advises the young officer, crossing his elbows over the newspapers littering his desk, all the Athens dailies, the Thessalonica dailies, the Alexandroupolis dailies, the local Orestiada rag, it's crazy all the newspapers that people still read in Greece: huge wads of pages wrapped in cellophane with gifts of CD-ROMs: *The Greek Temples*; *Alexander the Great's Great Battles*; *How to Furnish your Holiday Home*; *The Italian Cars of your Dreams*.

Agent Evangelos left his hotel to go directly to the police station, and now he hears the lieutenant saying, "Let it drop!" But the young policeman's familiar tone doesn't even surprise him; he finds it quite natural, he doesn't take it as a lack of respect, for at this stage in their collaboration formality is no longer appropriate.

"Just let it drop, Evangelos! They're happy in Athens, do you understand what I'm saying? Take it from me, the wall is the only thing that interests them, the only thing that matters to them, so they're leaving the case of the head to us, because they know we've no time to investigate further with all the migrants flooding in. On top of that, Frontex is likely to be working at half speed for a few days, and after the girl has talked, when she's told us where she's from, you can contact her embassy and she'll be on the first plane out."

"A plane to where?"

Agent Evangelos knows perfectly well what the lieutenant is saying, and he knows he is right. The directorate doesn't want the business of the severed head to get out because they're afraid the case will delay the construction of the wall.

"With this brothel business we're offering them a golden opportunity to bugger Frontex," adds Lieutenant

Anastasis. "My boss, the captain, hasn't recovered from it yet. If only you'd seen his face just now, when he saw the papers!"

"I'm going to see that girl in her cell right away," says Evangelos.

"The girl won't say anything today either, she's completely wiped out, and if it was up to me I'd let her leave, seeing that in any case the matter of the head is no longer of interest to your bosses in Athens."

For a moment, Agent Evangelos imagines the girl outside. "Outside where? In the streets of Orestiada, with no papers, no money, nothing, like all those poor folk you register every day and to whom you then say, 'Outside!'?"

"Yes, if you like, except that she comes from somewhere, not like the migrants who come from nowhere – you know what I mean. She has a country, she has the first plane home waiting for her, and she'll eventually tell us where she comes from."

"From which country?"

"From one of those goddamn countries in Eastern Europe."

Now Agent Evangelos, who had been standing with his back against the cold wall of the police station, goes across to the lieutenant: he plants his hands on the desk and brings his face close to the young officer, who smells of cigarette and coffee. "Lieutenant, do you remember what we said to one another, you and me, that time in the car?"

Lieutenant Anastasis shrugs.

"You know what you said to me?"

"In the absence of justice, the truth," the officer had said. He remembers all right, but he doesn't want to think about it; he takes a bunch of keys from a drawer.

"The truth; you committed to discovering the truth."

"I did, but where is all this getting us, Agent Evangelos?"

"To understanding, Lieutenant."

"To understanding what?"

"To understanding how."

"How what, Agent Evangelos?"

"How Greece has come to this."

To reach the cells in the Orestiada police station you have to go along the narrow corridor that passes by Lieutenant Anastasis's windowless office. Agent Evangelos is observing the girl through the spyhole. She is lying on the bench in the foetal position. Is she asleep? Tomorrow morning he'll take her to Athens. They'll take the plane from Alexandroupolis together.

Agent Evangelos won't have seen the river, nor will he have seen the existing few metres of barbed-wire wall, but he's not even thinking about that any longer. His daughter is doing well, his little granddaughter is doing very well. He has just called, and they'll soon be back home. It's a warm day outside; the depression moving down from the Balkans and covering all of Greece has shifted to the west, and winter seems to have given way to summer.

The streets of Athens are clogged with traffic like before the Olympic Games, like before the Metro. The public services are on strike; Syntagma Square is afloat in a pale mist; people are spitting on the foam-covered pavements; the tear gas is subsiding, spreading now into the Metro corridors. Dustbins are burning in front of the Polytechnic gates, where young people have taken refuge, ski masks at the ready. In Athens, masked rioters are advancing. At this hour of the day – it is almost noon – the faceless insurgents must be preparing a new stock of Molotov cocktails to be lined up in the corridors in front of the lecture rooms now converted into an entrenched encampment, and where for quite some time now not a single student was to be encountered, according to the colleagues who have infiltrated the various anarchist factions. Soon, when the confrontations with the riot police begin, the centre of Athens will become a battlefield. The Molotov cocktails will answer the tear gas.

Agent Evangelos knows perfectly well that there are no students in the Polytechnic. He also knows that there are no more anarchists in Greece, and is perfectly aware that his colleagues disguised as anarchists deserve the name no less than the young people in ski masks who claim to be anarchists but know nothing about anarchism and no longer know who they really are – just as he no longer knows either, like his colleagues sent in to spy, just as no one here in Greece knows any longer what uniform to wear.

This morning, only Agent Evangelos's daughter seems to know who she is. She must be the only one for whom motherhood and her apartment in Kifissia are the centre of the universe.

Somewhere in Athens, another young woman is completely lost. She was told yesterday evening that she was in a military clinic over towards Agia Paraskevi. She has been asked to state her identity and undergo a battery of medical tests. It turns out that in addition to Russian, Polina Zubov, born in Vladivostok on 9 January 1988, speaks quite good English. A student of languages in Russia, the young woman also has a few rudiments of Greek, learned during her numerous fortnight-long visits to Greece, working as an escort until she was dropped by her agency a month ago.

In the utterly chaotic state of Greece, a number of foreign girls turn to prostitution, most of them undeclared aliens. Like Polina, the great majority of those who work in the major hotels, where they pretend to be tourists, come from eastern Europe, mostly Russia and the Ukraine, Romania and Bulgaria. Evangelos has already questioned some of them. Sometimes his men require them to provide information on suspects. Some of these young women work in the countless unsavoury hotels in the large Greek cities. Each has a different story to tell. But the usual starting point is in their country of origin. Whether wishing to earn a lot of money as quickly as possible, or crippled by debt, or single mothers, or sometimes just wanting to help out their families, they don't hesitate to come to Greece to sell their bodies. They turn to agencies which organize their journeys and manage their agenda, starting with putting their profiles and photos on the appropriate websites. In the worst of cases, after working for a few months for one or another of these agencies, they will be kidnapped, raped and beaten by pimps from another agency to which they have been "sold", like ordinary merchandise, by the prostitution network that initially employed them. Agent Evangelos has lost count of the cases of girls entrapped by phoney employment agencies who promise them a dream job in Greece. But those girls skip working in a hotel: as soon as they arrive in Athens their passports are taken from them and they are confined to brothels. The pimps threaten to harm their families if they run away or resist – a highly efficient form of pressure. In the capital, as in other large Greek cities, African women represent the other extreme in sex trafficking. Often very young, manipulated and forced into prostitution in mostly insalubrious locations, or condemned to streetwalking on Patission Street, they are some of the most destitute among the prostitutes. And then there are the boys, very young ones, including young Afghans aged fifteen or sixteen, posted to solicit at the exit from the Metro on Omonoia Square under the vigilant eye of pimps who pick them up on their clandestine arrival in Greece. But that is another story.

The questioning of Polina has begun. She says that she picked up the axe, which was sitting on the running board of a piece of agricultural machinery among a heap of other tools, but it was the axe she picked up, she remembers, overcome by rage when she saw this man coming towards her. She heard him yell something like "No, don't do that!", but she was in a fury, and since she was holding the axe in one hand, just one hand, it was too heavy, she gripped her makeshift weapon with the other hand, and raised her arms holding it in both hands, but something seems to have stopped her. Something was hindering her. Was there some sort of obstacle? The axe remained poised in the air.

Agent Evangelos doesn't push her. Polina has to start over from the beginning.

"Polina, where were you when the agency dropped you?"

Polina speaks quietly. Her eyes are losing their wariness, no longer seeking an escape. They agree to restart the film of events, leaving it to Agent Evangelos to press the pause button on certain scenes.

Agent Evangelos and Polina are face to face. An hour after landing at Eleftherios Venizelos Airport, immediately after being transported at high speed along the flanks of Mount Hymettus in a special van with flashing blue lights, she entered a hospital ward reserved for officers' wives. A few minutes later she was informed in English of her rights and about the interrogation that would follow. She agreed with a nod, the first evidence of her apparent willingness to communicate, though she still hadn't uttered a word, remaining prostrate and silent during the entire drive from Orestiada to Alexandroupolis, and equally silent hunched in her seat during the entire flight to Athens. Though, as Agent Evangelos notes, she casts him a grateful look whenever he allows her to go to the toilet, which she did three times in Alexandroupolis Airport: twice in the plane, and once again on arriving in Athens.

"So, Polina, when did the agency drop you? Where were you?"

"I was in my room in the President Hotel when the manager called me. He said I was finished, and looking on my computer I found that my picture was gone from the escort sites. He said I wasn't getting enough customers and that I'd been given a bad review on one of the sites, claiming I wasn't doing everything it said on my ad. I can't understand that, because my customers were always satisfied, they gave me little presents, there was even one who asked me to dinner after a visit in my room. We went to eat in a nice restaurant, I thought it was very kind."

"Wait, Polina, hold on, not so fast. The 'manager', you say. Who is this individual?"

"The manager, my manager, is the person who tells me where I have to go."

"Can you tell me his name? Do you know it?"

"He's called Yuri; he's the one who tells me if I'm going to Athens, and for how long. Also, I think he was angry with me because I told him I didn't want to go to Thessalonica."

"You know nothing about him, you've never seen him?"

"No, he lives in Crete, we always talk by phone, and I was afraid to go to Thessalonica because the girls there work for the Mafia."

"For the Mafia?"

"Yes, they work for Mafia guys, and I think my manager is friends with the Mafia. There are girls like that who disappeared there, girls who hoped to work independently, came on their own to Greece, and who put their pictures on websites themselves without saying anything to the manager, and they disappeared."

"Let's backtrack for a moment, Polina. How did you join this agency?"

"I was living in Moscow. I had just finished my language courses. I wanted to buy a little apartment, but I knew it would take me years before I'd have the money. Then a girlfriend told me about this agency that sends girls to Greece. I went to an office and I was interviewed by a woman who explained it all to me. There was a contract to sign, with all the details. Then I took part in a photography session in a big Moscow hotel. I knew what it meant, working as an escort, but I was getting ahead, earning ten years' money in two years. That's the way it started. I went to Greece for the first time, and it all went according to plan. I had to stay in such-and-such a hotel and wait for clients to call me on the phone provided by the agency. Every morning a guy came to pick up the money. We were only allowed to accept cash, always euros. Then the agency deposited my share in a bank account, and I paid for the hotel with a credit card. When I talked to my parents by phone I told them I was in Moscow, though I was really in Athens. It was tough to start with, but I soon learned what to do. When a customer asked me if I enjoyed being with him, I'd smile and close my eyes, and he'd believe me. You just had to find the right words and what you did happened automatically."

"Polina, how long would you stay in Athens, usually?"

"Two weeks, sometimes just one, like these past months when there were fewer customers, because of the crisis."

"One more thing. In Athens, did you always work in big hotels?"

"Yes, in the President or the Park. I wasn't afraid at all, for there are lots of people around and you can always call reception; the hotel staff are nice, they know very well what you're doing but they don't say anything, and they give you a wink on your way out."

"I think you said you'd called a client the evening the agency fired you."

"That's right, that evening I felt uneasy at the idea of going to Thessalonica. I thought the manager was angry, and I felt all alone in my room, and then I called a customer I liked a lot, the one who'd invited me to dinner. I'd kept his phone number and his first name; he'd told me to call him Peter but I don't know if it was his real name, though it suited him well. When he answered my call, he seemed surprised to hear me, but he seemed like a person I could talk to, so I told him I was bored all on my own. I was scared to go out, because I don't like Athens very much, for the men in the street just give you funny looks. The customer was so sorry, he was just about to leave Greece, so I wished him a good trip, and then felt all lonely in my room again. OK, it's true I wasn't getting a lot of customers compared with the previous times I was in Greece. But it wasn't my fault, there's a crisis happening and I was getting fewer calls on my mobile, but I don't understand why they dropped me like that. I didn't want to go home to Moscow, but on the other hand I didn't want to keep paying for the room in the President, a hotel completely lacking in charm."

Agent Evangelos takes note of "completely lacking in charm". It may be true, of course, but he quite likes the multi-storey hotel, its massive bulk visible from afar, towering over the district of Ambelokopi, probably because of his recollection of the time he went there to pick up his uncle from America, his mother's elder brother. Evangelos had waited in the foyer, in front of the leather armchairs, formal in his suit; he'd come to meet the old man and bring him to his parents' house, one Sunday around noon. As he entered through the President's sliding doors he told himself that the United States must resemble this: the vast foyer, the different levels, the few steps and a ramp leading to the lifts, the staircases, broad accesses to the lower floors that plunged into the basement like on the photos of the Grand Central Terminal in New York, and the conference rooms whose noticeboards announced the "60th Anniversary of the Melbourne Greek Association" or an "International Symposium on Hydrocarbon Resources in the Aegean Sea". His uncle walked behind him, and Evangelos could see the two of them in the endless mirror of the bar to their left as they went, leaving the smell of filter coffee and bacon and eggs behind them and emerging from a decor that was still novel in Athens, with the city fragmented and rearranged into cubes in the reflection from its windows of smoked glass.

Not "lacking in charm" then, the President, but it's true the hotel can't be unchanged. Yet Agent Evangelos can well imagine himself waiting there for Polina, and seeing her emerge from the lift. He can see himself crossing the foyer with Polina on his arm, like that Peter who takes her out to dinner, she clinging to his arm and he feeling a slight pressure from her hand as if to say that she won't make a nuisance of herself, that they mustn't forget that this is all just a game. And then dinner in a restaurant in Kolonaki, Polina wearing a simple pullover and jeans – Evangelos imagines her in a little cream-coloured leather jacket; only her belt is a little ostentatious, with its buckle bearing the emblem of an Italian brand. She sits very upright on her chair in the restaurant, fending off the world with her smile. Her nose, eyes, blonde hair, are all perfectly matched: the nose is perfect, the eyes too, the mouth is fine, but that's not at all surprising since Polina doesn't talk much, and her smile isn't evasive, as you might remark too hastily – no, it's just an invisible thread that makes him aware of the distance. Now she's taking her time reading the menu, finally choosing just a mozzarella salad and saying to Peter, "I wouldn't mind having a little white wine, but just a glass," and he laughing as he imagines her losing control for a moment; Peter is relaxed, sensing that she appreciates the occasion; she's not as mechanical as in the bedroom a while ago; she's here, not behaving like a hooker any more. Poor fellow, do we have to maintain this illusion of crossing the invisible frontier separating us from this young Russian woman; a glass, just a glass of white: apparently Polina always wants to stay in control, as Agent Evangelos is beginning to understand.

Agent Evangelos is listening to Polina, who now says, "So since I didn't want to stay at the President, a hotel lacking in charm, and seeing as I didn't have too much money left either, and I didn't want to leave Athens without earning something, I began sending messages to friends in Russia who also work as escorts, and I remembered a girl from Vladivostok who does the same as me, her name is Olga, she works for another agency that might have taken me on, though I don't think that one is much good. Olga never answered my calls, but she told me in a text message that she had mentioned me to them; she was on Mykonos, an island in Greece, she told me. Two hours later she sent me a phone number I should call. A guy who spoke Russian answered. He arranged to meet me in another hotel in Athens, the Lacoba. I got ready, I packed my bag and I went there by taxi."

"Where did you stay?"

Agent Evangelos thinks he knows where the Lacoba is, one of those "love hotels" that exist by the dozen in Athens, offering a room at twenty-two euros for three hours, anonymity guaranteed, you pay cash, there's no trace: you leave with your girlfriend, a student like yourself, and go with her to her parents' house; you leave with your lover, no one is any the wiser; you exit on your own, leaving the hooker alone in the room to get dressed; sometimes you leave the hotel holding your head down, with your wife, yes that's who she is, you leave very nonchalantly and go home to the children, for there's no privacy in your two-room apartment.

"Where did you say, to the Lacoba? That must be the hotel at the bottom of Syngrou Avenue, behind a big hospital. Do you remember the address?"

No, Polina just knows that the taxi knew right away where it was, and it was just now when Agent Evangelos asked her to describe the route it took to the Lacoba that she managed to remember: "Yes, it took a kind of motorway in the middle of town, towards the sea, and then turned to the right." She knows too that there was a large deserted entrance foyer with only a young woman at the reception desk, who gave her the keys to a room on the fifth floor. And when she got out of the lift she was surprised to hear moans, women's voices, laughter, men's voices too, but mostly women, exclamations, little cries, well, she's not going to join the dots, you know what it is!

Agent Evangelos asks Polina to think carefully about what she's saying. She mustn't forget anything, she mustn't lie. He reminds her that she doesn't have the right to remain silent, that she can't ask for a lawyer, since this isn't the usual kind of interrogation. She has to understand fully that she must tell the truth and really describe everything in the slightest detail.

So, yes, Polina was surprised to hear so many women enjoying sex in the nearby rooms, you could hear everything, there was also a sound like lashes from a whip, at intervals, but regularly, and waiting there in the room all by herself, sitting on a big bed with a large white sheet stretched over it, waiting in her room listening to those cries from the other side of the walls covered with mirrors, seeing herself there all alone in the mirrors, in the room lit by little red and yellow bulbs, waiting in this very immaculate place, now, long after the cries and the voices stopped, Polina could hear the noise of a vacuum cleaner in the room with the whip, and then there came the dull thumps of a mop against the corridor door, still all alone, smelling the cleaning product, hearing steps, a door closing, then more little cries and moans that became louder and louder. Polina decided to call reception to ask if they might have something to eat. And it was later, when she'd finished her grilled ham and cheese sandwich and had finally fallen asleep on the bed, her face lit by the glow of the porno film playing on the big screen above the bed, it was a while later that the man knocked on her room door.

Polina says he was Greek; he spoke no Russian, it wasn't the person on the phone.

"He only spoke Greek, and he signed to me to follow him. I pretended not to understand, and that's when he slapped my face."

Agent Evangelos would like to know more about this individual, but he can see that Polina has had enough, he knows well that this rape is the first of many, he knows, he can imagine the distress and the fear. He asks the young woman if she can tell him how long it lasted, she must tell him if it was five minutes or an hour, whether the man allowed her some time or if he took her to the parking lot immediately afterwards, whether they met anyone in the corridor, and if she cried out or called for help.

No, Polina was so scared that she didn't dare call for help; she cried out at first, but behind the mirrors, in the other rooms, there were other cries, and no one was surprised to hear cries, and even beatings with a belt like was done to her, and also because she herself had heard something like lashes from a whip earlier on after she arrived at the Lacoba, and because of all that she had no choice, in that hotel where you could hear all kinds of things going on and anything could happen.

"Then," says Polina, "he told me to follow him, I had no time to go to the bathroom, I had to follow him, he dragged me by the arm, we went down in the lift directly to the parking garage in the basement."

"There was no one in the parking garage?" asks Evangelos.

"No, there was no one around, and he pushed me into a little bus where there were three other girls, all crying. There were two men waiting: one was the driver, he spoke Russian, and there was another man who spoke both Russian and Greek; he exchanged a few words with the one from the room, but he didn't get into the bus with us."

"What then?"

"After that we went out, or, rather, the bus left the underground parking and drove just a few minutes to another building, like a big garage with lorries and offices upstairs. There they told us to get out and locked us in a room; we waited for an hour, about an hour I think, and they did let us go to the bathroom. They gave us water to drink too, and after that I don't remember anything. I think they gave us a drug to make us sleep, because when I woke up we were driving. It was dark night, and there was no window, I could hardly breathe, my tongue was heavy, it stank of vomit, with the other girls, about twenty of us I think, we were packed into the back of a lorry, as I saw when they opened the doors. We drove like that for hours and hours with the other girls, we were all throwing up. And I was really scared, I was afraid I'd throw up

117

again because I was taking medicine for my kidneys, and since I didn't have my bag any more I was scared, but now I'm used to the pain that has come back, and it's there all the time."

Agent Evangelos asks what medicine she was taking, and briefly interrupts the interview to dial a number on a wall phone. "Yes, Zyloprim, she hasn't taken any for weeks. Yes, that's it, Zyloprim; do what you can to find some."

"But tell me," Agent Evangelos resumes, "don't you remember any details – I mean when you were in that big building with the lorries?"

Polina only remembers a name written in large Roman letters: Orpheus.

"But that's very important," says Agent Evangelos, "you mustn't forget a single thing if you want us to get anywhere. So, where was this name written?"

"I read the name Orpheus when we arrived in front of the building, there was a big sign on the roof saying Orpheus, and I think the same thing was written on the lorry that brought us."

Agent Evangelos typed this part of Polina's story on his computer, as far as she managed to tell it. He put it in chronological order, starting with the President Hotel: the President, the Lacoba, the short bus ride, the stop at the headquarters of Orpheus Tarminoglou (which turned out to be a transport company based in Kallithea, owned by a member of Golden Dawn, the extreme right-wing party), the trip in the lorry, and the Eros brothel. As for what followed, Evangelos said to himself, 'I'll see about the rest tomorrow, but I think I'll pay a visit to my daughter and then go to the Batman; I've been thinking of it for days now.' In fact Evangelos thinks of it constantly, and going there will help him to think more clearly. But the thing is that the story is forthcoming, and it can't wait.

Polina resumes her story when Agent Evangelos invites her to, after first ordering a coffee, using the wall phone for the second time.

"A coffee?"

"No thanks, I don't drink coffee. And after that they made us go into that house beside the road; they ordered us to sit on the ground and told us that nothing would happen to us if we were nice to the people who'd come to pay us a visit. They gave us Coke to drink. It tasted strange, and that's when they drugged us. Almost right away I felt I was no longer myself, like I was drunk. And that's when the guys came. They spoke German and English and other languages I didn't recognize. Those guys made us crazy, and they laughed to see us crazy like that. They ripped our clothes, and they made fun of us when we tried to scratch and bite them. I don't know what came over us. We were like crazy, we fought with them, but that's what they wanted, they wanted us to hit them and bite them. I swear to you, I've never been as naked in my life, I had no control of myself any more, I couldn't even recognize my own reflection, something had driven me out of my own skin…"

"And then?" asked Agent Evangelos.

"Then nothing. I keep telling myself I should never have phoned that customer who calls himself Peter, I should never have left the President Hotel with him; I let him see me just the way I am, I wasn't Alisa Model any more – that was the name I used on the agency website. As I said, they must have been spying on me, because as soon as I was back in the hotel after spending the evening with this Peter without asking him for anything, my false name was gone off the agency website. And that's how I came to phone this guy who arranged to meet me at the Lacoba. If I'd never called his number none of all this would have happened."

Agent Evangelos checked: Alisa Model had not been online for at least three months. However, the people in IT were able to recover the escort's profile:

> Alisa Model
> AGE: 23
> HEIGHT: 172 cm (5'8")
> WEIGHT: 52 kg (115 lb)
> BODY: 91–61–92 cm (36–24–36")
> BREASTS: C
> HAIR COLOUR: Blonde
> NATIONALITY: Russian
> LANGUAGES: Russian
> English
> Greek (some)

Agent Evangelos asks Polina to pick up her story at the point where she was tempted to run away from the Eros brothel. "You were holding that axe, and you told me that it was as if someone had stopped you from bringing it down —"

"Yes, that's right, someone stopped me from using the axe."

"Someone?"

"I don't know who."

"But let's not go so fast, Polina," says Agent Evangelos, picking up the thread of her statement. "You told me you had never felt as naked as you did during those weeks you spent in the Eros brothel."

"Yes, I was lost, scared to death, I no longer knew who I was, what I was like. I just wanted to be an escort, but now it had all turned into a nightmare. The other girls and I were just there, somewhere, in a room with no windows, lying on mattresses laid directly on a strange floor, waiting for passing customers, dreadful men, soldiers who spoke all kinds of languages. But that was nothing compared with the days when we had to put on a kind of white nightdress and wear wreaths on our heads, the days when they forced us to drink that bitter-tasting drug mixed with Coke."

Agent Evangelos asked Polina if she really had no idea of the place where she'd been kept, and her only response was in the form of pictures.

"There was a field in front, with trees farther off."

"You had no other way to tell where you were?"

"No, I knew I was in the middle of nowhere, beyond anything I could imagine."

"Could you repeat that?"

"I could never have imagined anything like it," Polina repeats.

Agent Evangelos next asks her if the men who came to the brothel wore uniforms.

"Yes, most of them," says Polina. "I could see them undressing before they began to drink and make us dance for them. They pushed us into a kind of invisible circle; I remember that everything was spinning, there was very loud techno music, and they made us spin and spin, they pulled our hair, they pinched us, they tripped us up, until we became crazed with fury."

"And then one day, that day – that night, I mean – tell me again what happened?" Evangelos presses her.

He instantly believes every word that Polina Zubov utters after that. Because you can't make up a story like that. And because he was firmly convinced, from that moment when he met the young woman's gaze for the first time in the Orestiada police station, that this person wasn't wearing a mask: displacement was the only evidence of her existence.

"So, that evening, as you said, you ran from the brothel, pursued by one of those men?"

"The man who chased me," says Polina, "was one of the customers – not the soldier, but someone I'd often seen there and who was very familiar with the men who guarded us. I even wondered if he wasn't one of their bosses. He was very brutal, and he enjoyed hurting me, he used to pinch me very hard, he used to hit me."

"And so you found yourself outside?"

"I don't think I knew what I was doing, and I even wondered if I'd had a flash of awareness, as if I felt I was going to die from exhaustion, from the dancing and howling."

"Do you realize what you're saying?" interrupts Agent Evangelos, for he knows how this possible flash of

awareness on Polina's part could have disastrous conse-
quences for her, occurring as it did in a sequence of events
which until that point had occurred entirely beyond her
control, under the influence of a drug-induced hysteria.

But Polina isn't aware of anything; she's tired of repeating what she has already described.

"Then I found myself behind the building, on the side
next to the road, where they hang out our sheets – if you
can call them that – that never dry, after they were washed
in a tub; that's where they dry, behind the fence, and I
got tangled in them, I fell down among the wet sheets. I
could feel that guy grabbing me by the leg, but I threw
the sheet in his face. I got up, and that's when I saw the
axe, it was sitting there on some farm machine, and when
I turned around I saw a man's face; he was shouting 'No,
don't!' And then I no longer had the axe in one hand,
because it was heavy, so I'd taken it in both hands, and I
was trying to strike when I felt that someone had taken
me by the arm and was stopping me."

"So there were two men?"

"I don't know who the man was that shouted 'No,
don't!' I don't remember seeing him before, but I know
he was shouting."

"In what language, Polina?"

"I can't remember now, but it wasn't Greek, or English,
or Russian, I don't know any more."

"But according to you he said, 'No, don't!', so you must
have understood what he was saying."

"Yes, but I don't know any more what language he was
speaking, and since I'm telling you that he shouted out

'No!', and afterwards it was like I wasn't about to bring down the axe, for it felt like someone was holding back one of my arms, like my action was stopped."

"Yet you saw the head fall?"

"No, no, I didn't see it fall, it was just a few seconds later, when the noise had stopped, after the soldiers came out. They pulled on their trousers, but their chests were bare, and it was then they found me, and I could see the terror in their eyes, and I followed where they were looking, and the head was right there, at my feet, and they went back, and that's how I was able to get away and run off into the dark."

"But your clothes" – Agent Evangelos has only thought of this now – "you say they were forcing you to wear a kind of white nightdress, isn't that so? You told me several times that you had to wear a kind of costume for the orgies, so why were you found in street clothes, wearing a sweater and jeans?"

"Because that evening there weren't a lot of customers, so I just tried to run away, I lied to you."

The young woman looks at Agent Evangelos, who repeats to himself, 'Because I lied to you, because Polina is lying, like Alisa Model, like my directorate lies, like the frontier guards lie, like the migrants lie under questioning, like I lie to myself, like everyone here in Greece tells lies.'

Evangelos could have continued the interview. But a question has occurred to him, though he doesn't know exactly why.

"What do you know about the crisis, Polina?"

"What?"

"Yes, you said you had fewer customers because of the crisis. What did you mean by that?"

"There were fewer men calling, because of the crisis."

"Yes, I understand, I understand perfectly. But what do you know about the crisis in Greece?"

"One day, I was in the Park Hotel, and I heard shouts and explosions coming from the street. I went out to see what was happening and I saw people everywhere. There was a demonstration going on, and young people were fighting the police. I watched the news on TV, and I heard lots of people saying that the whole thing, the crisis, was just a fiction."

"Meaning what, a 'fiction'?"

"That's what they say on TV, the Greeks, they say the crisis is just a fiction, something that doesn't really exist. I don't know... something made up."

"And you, Polina, what do you think?"

"They say the crisis is just in people's heads, and I think they're right."

Episode III

Alisa Model has disappeared. David Minc, a financial expert born in Paris in 1973, is upset. He has had a long day: the liquidation of ATEbank (a drifting Greek wreck) is dragging on, the sessions with the bank directors have been interminable, and the prospect of having to do without the services of his little Russian is rousing his stomach pains again. Dammit, where can she have got to, the little minx? She has disappeared from the radar of athensescorts.gr, the go-to sex site in Athens from which David Minc, the first day of his assignment in Greece, had ferreted her out after hours of night-time surfing from his room at the Divani Caravel Hotel.

Alisa Model has been expunged from the map of Athens, and Polina Zubov won't be returning to Greece, having been barred from the country despite her protests. She is to take a plane to Moscow the following day, at one in the afternoon. Agent Evangelos has tried to make her see that she is getting off lightly, for in normal times she would have had more problems because her statement barely hangs together, and that she can consider herself lucky that no one else is taking any interest in her case, starting with the directorate, which prefers to concentrate on the Frontex business, displaying its contempt for the truth even when the national interest is at stake, even if it means closing the file on Polina. But Evangelos keeps all this to himself while resolving to pursue the inquiry for his own satisfaction, in collaboration with Lieutenant Anastasis, to whom he has sent the description of the man Polina had described once she decided to stop spinning yarns and relate what really happened that evening in the Eros brothel when that head was chopped off by the stroke of an axe that she wasn't holding, according to her story at least.

At this moment, Polina is spending her last night in a bedroom of the Sofitel Athens Airport, awaiting deportation. Now that she is locked in, with a policeman posted in the corridor, Agent Evangelos turns off the bedside lamp in a nearby room and closes his eyes. But he can still hear Polina lamenting the loss of everything she had – her agency and her regular customers – as well as the fact that she doesn't know in which European city she will be able to find work. Agent Evangelos remains silent, listening to her. He understands, he imagines her return to Moscow, the complete lack of resources that awaits her there, her mother's phone call enquiring if she has had a nice holiday and saying that her father would like her to come home to Vladivostok for Easter, and Polina looking for new contacts as she tries to find work in Europe, still determined to buy that apartment.

"But doesn't this experience – I mean what you've gone through here in Greece – doesn't all that abominable treatment make you want to get out of the sex trade?"

Agent Evangelos would have liked to tell Polina what he could have said to the Pakistani waiting at the traffic light with his squeegee and bucket of soapy water: Why do you keep on, here, breathing in the exhaust fumes; why, despite all the poverty?

Polina knows she won't always be so lucky, that eventually her luck could run out, that it has been costly for her, body and soul, yet she won't give up her dream of that little apartment in Moscow, of building herself a different world, a refuge where she can work everything out, make a new beginning and (why not?) start a family – but it will be up to her to decide with whom, and she'll owe her husband nothing. Only then will she pay a visit to her parents at Easter, when she's as round as a balloon and living in her own place in Moscow. Polina didn't express it in precisely those terms, but it amounts to the same thing when she says that Agent Evangelos must understand that it's a hard job, but that it means everything to her and she can't imagine just admitting defeat, so if it isn't Athens it'll be some other big city.

A short time ago, on the way to the airport, before joining Polina, who was already shut in her hotel room, Agent Evangelos told himself that he would pay a visit to his daughter and granddaughter. And now that he thinks about it, as he reclines on a king-size bed in the usual tomb of a standard room in the bubble of the airport Sofitel, he reflects that the little girl does really look like her grandmother, his former wife – but it's still too soon to say, and anyway Andromeda is sure that her little nose will grow a lot and become more like her maternal grandfather's, Agent Evangelos's – but, after all, what difference does it make? The most amazing thing of all was the unchanged atmosphere of Kifissia, with its shopping streets as smooth as tennis courts, its heated terraces, its news stands flanked by humidors set at the proper temperature – the fashionable neighbourhood of Kifissia with its stay-at-home mothers bored out of their minds in their expensive pyjamas, its fathers absently reading the news of the riots devastating the distant city centre, the Filipino maids laden with groceries, and all that coffee, all that fresh orange juice, all those shoes, very expensive cars, cigarettes, pastries, perfumes, beauty products, painted nails and high heels – how can such a hill of garbage still remain standing at the edge of the Athenian cesspool?

Agent Evangelos is a grandfather, the light hasn't been turned off in the toilet of the Sofitel bedroom; is little Polina asleep already? But no, of course, she won't close an eye all night, for she knows her hours here are now numbered – no more than a dozen hours left in Greece before she emerges into the corridor without handcuffs, as had been agreed, given the minimal risk of flight; and anyway, where could she go? The silent, windowless corridor of the Sofitel – the room doors all closed, like at the President, like in every hotel, like at the Hilton and the Divani Caravel where at the moment the top officials of the Troika are masturbating in front of their tablets, deprived of their Alisa Model, too tired to go and get laid in the President – the corridor, the lift, and then the direct descent into the underground parking where a black van awaits her, like at the Lacoba, but she's no longer thinking about that, she wants to stay here, in Athens, and wait in other hotel rooms, open her door to other customers, new ones, to take her clothes off, to be naked, to close her eyes when they touch her, to pretend, to take her usual precautions, always "with", even if the site says she'll do it "without"; she closes her eyes, says nothing, submits, shifts her position, turns over, looks away. She doesn't want to get into this vehicle that is to drive her directly to the plane; she doesn't want to go back to Russia, not like this, not penniless, with nothing, and then what will she do in Moscow?

Agent Evangelos believes Polina Zubov, he knows she's telling the truth, but it's a truth of interest to no one in Athens, a city that is ever prey to fresh "episodes", to a popular upsurge against fresh economic measures, while his superiors create a diversion with the Frontex affair.

On the other hand, he isn't especially convinced by that other fact uttered by the young Russian woman:

"There was a man outside, he was tangled in the sheets hanging out to dry, I don't know what he was doing there. I'd got dressed to escape from that place. I wanted to run away, I'd seized the opportunity while the guard was absent, the one who kept watch on us. On my way out, I found an axe, and thought I could use it to defend myself, if I had to. And when I saw this guy standing there, tangled in the sheets, for a moment I took him for another guard, a new one, like the ones that came from time to time, but then I saw him, the other one, the jerk, the one I'd seen over the previous days, always looking at us with his filthy expression, a dirty bastard who slapped me all the time when we had to take part in those orgies, I saw him appear out of the shadows, behind the one caught in the sheets. Then I raised the axe and rushed at them, at the two of them, I must have been yelling, I think I was yelling. But that's when everything goes black inside my head. I can see the stranger taking me by the arm and shouting, 'No! No!' And I was trying to strike the other one, the jerk; I was trying to hit him with the axe. The stranger shouldn't have tried to stop me, he shouldn't have but that's the way it was, that's how it happened, he shouldn't have, because that bastard that used to slap me, a regular in the brothel, he rushed at the stranger, shoved him to the ground and picked up the axe, for I'd dropped it, and tried to hit him with it; it looked like he wanted to kill him. But the stranger fought back; he grabbed the madman holding the axe by the leg and pulled him down. The jerk was on the ground, he was wild with anger, he tried to break loose, and then I saw them struggling, rolling one on top of the other in the sheets, on the terrace, and suddenly the dirty bastard stood up, and he was holding the axe, and he raised it to hit the guy on the ground. That's when I kicked him in the back, and it threw him forward. The other one took his chance to grab the axe, and struck him with it."

"Do you know if he was deliberately aiming at his neck?"

"I don't know. I just remember that the head didn't come off right away. It was later," says Polina, "when we were dragging the guard's body to the little path beside the brothel. There we were, that man and me dragging the body, and that's when the head came off, and I just know that the stranger had blood all over his clothes. He said something to me, it was in Greek, yes, I think it was Greek, he spoke to me, and I didn't understand at all; he pointed at the head, I can see myself there, I was scared, so was he, and he waved to me to run. He went on dragging the body without its head, he pulled it along by the feet, like a sack of potatoes. I followed him to the river, and that's where he abandoned the guard's body in a ditch, and then both of us walked very fast across the fields, to a little disused railway station. We waited there a few hours, until dawn. When the sun – well, you know, the light, the morning – that was when the man said to me in English, 'Wait! Wait!' I was supposed to wait for him, he said something like 'Hotel, hotel,' but I didn't see him for a few hours, and then he came back looking for me. He'd changed his clothes. We returned to the road, where his car was parked. We drove to the outskirts of a little town where he'd booked two rooms in a motel, the Europa Motel, I'm sure of the name because the next night I looked at the neon sign flashing right in front of my window."

"Who was this man? Tell me what you know about him."

"He was nice, he never touched me, he didn't want anything from me, and he brought me things to eat during the few hours we spent there waiting. I was in shock, and so was he. He told me he was German and Greek."

Polina then pronounced a name that Agent Evangelos lost no time in communicating by text message to Lieutenant Anastasis: "Nikolaus, a German of Greek origin, suspect No. 1."

Polina continued talking.

"The man spoke to me, he told me he was thinking, that we'd leave the country together, but I didn't understand anything that was going on, I slept all the time; I had a fever. He went out the next morning. He told me to wait there, still speaking English. He'd come back, he said, he just needed to find another jacket, different clothes, and then we would leave in a rented car. He'd forgotten his mobile. At one point a text message came on it. I read it, and that was how I worked out his name was Nikolaus, because the message began with his name and ended with a question mark. That evening, seeing he wasn't coming back, I became frightened, and because I couldn't stand being shut in any longer either, I went outside and the night was pitch-black, and I walked, and that's how the police found me."

So that was how the police found Polina, and now Agent Evangelos believes her story because it hangs together neither better nor worse than all the ones reported on the TV news and on the front of the news stands, like the story about the debt, or the Frontex affair, or the ones about migrants – he has seen them, entire families in front of the Orestiada police station every morning.

'What can you believe in nowadays?' wonders Agent Evangelos. The legend of Orpheus, his head borne along by the waters of the Evros, still mourning his Eurydice? And who could believe that Evangelos had done his military service under the flag of the Colonels' Greece? Or believe that his grandmother had been thrown overboard from a ship at sea off Smyrna, in 1922? Or that an arms dealer named Barbaros finances every one of the Greek political parties in exchange for Athens renewing certain major arms contracts with Germany? Right now, Evangelos is sure of only one thing: he'll tell Andromeda, his daughter, that she shouldn't feel she's obliged to name the little girl after her two grandmothers, Eleni and Elena. Why does history always have to repeat itself? What if she gave her a different name?

The sky is cloudless over Attica, and if it weren't for all those lights around the airport the moon would stand out in the sky, but almost all that remains to draw attention to her are the distant flanks of Mount Hymettus. The last train to Corinth is leaving the station in front of the Sofitel; there's no more Metro, for tomorrow public transit will be on strike. Drivers are waiting in their yellow cabs. A plane from the United States has just landed; they'd like to smoke, but smoking is forbidden, and that's why they don't even listen to Greek music on the radio any more.

Tomorrow evening Agent Evangelos will be on a flight back north. He's going to get to the bottom of this case. Thanks to the information provided by Polina, he should be able to get his hands on that Nikolaus very soon. Even better, Lieutenant Anastasis has just sent him a message saying that he has found the fugitive's mobile in the hotel room where he'd gone to earth with Polina. The first name of the owner of the phone number is the one provided by the girl: Nikolaus, his full name is Nikolaus Strom. Anastasis mentioned something else: the last call received by Strom was from a certain Christina Lazaridou, a resident of Athens. Agent Evangelos will summon her to his office as soon as he has seen Polina onto the Moscow plane. It will be in Lazaridou's best interest to tell him everything she knows about Strom. It won't take Agent Evangelos long to locate the fugitive on the map of the Evros delta. When he does find him, they'll have a little chat together, and only then will Evangelos be able to return to the Batman for a drink. In the meantime, no one has claimed the dead body yet. That's odd! He'll have to phone the mufti. And tell him what, exactly? That his dead body isn't a good Muslim. If it was up to him, Agent Evangelos would pack the corpse back to Sidiro without further ado. He'll suggest it to Lieutenant Anastasis.

From the heights of Ekali, north of Athens, the capital is just a dull rumble borne on the roar of a motorbike along a fast road, somewhere on the plain of Attica. Sitting with his back to the half-open window of his office, Panos Barbaros doesn't even hear it. In his irritation, his entire attention is focused on the owl's cry.

When he decided to build his house in the middle of a formerly remote pine grove, Panos Barbaros didn't have the trees cut down, unlike his new neighbours, who are now too numerous in this upscale neighbourhood. Surrounded by trees, his house has remained shielded from prying eyes. Having been spared by wildfires, his property has always been inhabited by nocturnal creatures, among whom the owl reigns supreme. Its eyes, like the surveillance cameras dotted along the wall surrounding his vast domain, detect the slightest movement.

This evening, the bird's regular cries have been unable to calm Panos Barbaros's agitation. Something has upset him. It calls for an immediate reaction on his part. A man has died. And, unfortunately, he wasn't the one meant to die. Now the country is under threat. And since he, Panos Barbaros, is responsible for the security of Greece, it is up to him to act. This situation is even more irritating in that for some time now there have been a lot of red lights: Brussels doesn't want a wall on the Evros. Berlin continues to repeat that if Athens wants to strengthen its border security it will just have to pay for the means to keep out clandestine migrants itself.

Panos Barbaros is disappointed in Germany. Since the end of the Second World War his family has always maintained a special link with that country. His father, a doctor, a communist and member of the Epirus resistance, had been a Germanophile despite everything. Didn't he say to his son, "Don't confuse the Nazis with the Germans"? During the 1950s, when the hunt for communists in Greece became intolerable, his father moved the entire family to Berlin, where they lived until the end of the Colonels' regime in 1974. Among his German patients, Panos Barbaros's father counted numerous dignitaries, including a certain Erich Honecker. Ancient history, no doubt, but a history that still counts for something today.

Panos Barbaros completed his studies at the Athens Polytechnic nine years before the fall of the Berlin Wall. He already owned twelve shops selling electronic equipment in the major Greek cities. Ten years later he was the foremost provider of mobile phones in the country. And when he built a factory to manufacture batteries in the north of the country it was natural for him to start doing business with the Germans. It was equally logical for him to facilitate links between Athens and Berlin to enable the purchase of German military equipment by Greece. But since Angela Merkel came to power things had no longer been the same. Panos Barbaros had lost his direct line to the Ministry of Defence. His special contacts had been transferred to different departments, and it was as if, at a single stroke, the Greeks were no longer welcome in Germany. Otherwise, how could one explain Berlin's reticence towards the construction of the Greek wall? Panos Barbaros still can't get over it. Why would the Germans be opposed to European financing of a security measure for which the entire material would be supplied by companies belonging to his group? Berlin knows very well the considerable influence he wields in Athens. If Greece defends its eastern coastline with German submarines, it's thanks to him, Panos Barbaros. If Athens has never queried the arms contracts with Germany, it's not by chance. Who had persuaded successive Greek governments to buy German torpedoes? During election campaigns Panos Barbaros has always supported both the left and the right. Political campaigns are costly, and his discreet generosity has always been appreciated. In exchange for his support, Panos Barbaros has had no difficulty in extracting guarantees of military cooperation with Germany from the parties in power. Can Berlin have forgotten the services he has rendered?

But time is short. At this moment, a man who should be dead rather than another man is gadding about the country. He won't get far. 'But even after the police get their hands on him,' reflects Barbaros, 'he'll still be a threat to my wall.'

Outside, the owl has fallen silent. The moon is obscured by large clouds from off the sea. Panos Barbaros closes his eyes. However, he isn't sleeping. He is trying to visualize the frontier formed by the River Evros. He locates the spot where the river makes an elbow. That is where he is to unroll kilometres of barbed wire fitted with ultra-sophisticated electronic surveillance equipment. That is where a steel wall will be built, at whatever cost. No one is going to rob him of his wall.

An idea occurs to him. It isn't complete yet. But it will take shape eventually. He'll set some kind of trap. They'll all fall into it: the fugitive, the Germans, the Europeans – everybody who stands in the way of his security fence. By the morning, when the sun's first rays skim the pine forest, his plan will be clear. At seven he'll call the minister on his mobile. His instructions will be extremely precise.

Episode IV

That day, when he spoke her first name over the phone, Christina Lazaridou felt that soon she would be only a memory for him. When he said, "We can't go on," she wasn't surprised. At that precise moment, she could still have cut the ground from under him by answering, "If that's what you want." He'd have replied, like in the past, "Oh! But not at all! It's what we want, the two of us, we talked about it and you agreed."

Perhaps they'd have left it at that, and none of what followed would have occurred. Nikolaus – Nikos, as Christina calls him – wouldn't be in this mess. And she wouldn't have heard his name, Strom, spoken this morning, along with an urgent summons to meet the police. She wonders what he can have done. They had found her number on Nikos's mobile. They said her name was the only one listed on the speed dial. 'Has he kept our text messages?' she wonders. She's sure they've read the lot. She doesn't even know where Nikos is. And even if she did, she wouldn't tell them. 'If they accused you of something,' she thinks, 'I'd tell them it's impossible. You wouldn't harm anyone, and I don't see what you can be accused of.'

A year ago she had said nothing when Nikos told her he would be in Athens in three days' time. "In three days," he'd repeated, "and we must say goodbye, once for all, for all the times we've already tried, without really believing in it." She'd said nothing.

Christina goes over the scene in her mind. 'I could feel he was leaving. I let him go.' They would never have reached such a point if she hadn't remained silent. Christina had said nothing. For too long, she hasn't spoken. Words take time to come to her, and by the time they reach her lips they're already ineffectual. So she remains silent, as always. When she met Nikos, she remembers, 'he talked to me, he talked and talked, it was an uninterrupted stream, a developing narrative that he reeled off to me as if it was already written down and the time had come to recite it. We were on that balcony in Piraiki, and I was listening to him rather than seeing him.' Christina drank in his words, surprised to find she understood them. Only Nikos was talking. Already, true to form for her, she was saying nothing. But she must have been smiling, and in her smile he could read the only words that mattered right then. They wanted each other, and no translation was needed for them to understand.

He German, and she Greek, but the German so Greek – though a bit German nevertheless.

She can still hear him saying, "It's over between us!"

'And it's true,' she recognizes today. 'That was what we decided, and yet we knew very well it was only beginning.' Now it's all starting again. He is leaving her, and she is left to confront her silence.

Since Nikos's departure she has been trying to find the words she should have said. Then there are the ones she blames herself for uttering without thinking. Like that summer, in her grandfather's house, in their holiday home on Spetses. She had previously rejected the idea of bringing him there. She has never felt comfortable between those stone walls, in the neighbourhood overlooking the old port and the remnants of the naval dockyard that had enriched the island several centuries ago. The figure of her grandfather haunts the place; everything brings her back to those long August evenings when he would order his daughter, her mother, around. "So, what's become of that coffee? And what about the Turkish delight? And cut up the fruit, the oranges and the apples with cinnamon, you know I like them properly peeled, you know that, don't you?"

Her grandfather, born in Istanbul, with his dark glasses, now back in Greece, arriving one fine day bag and baggage from his city, accompanied by his new wife and their daughter, a voluntary exile at the age of seventy, having sold his property and disposed of the shops in Pera. A Greek native of Constantinople who for years had been unable to decide to leave his homeland, Turkey. She remembers how they went to Hellinikon Airport to welcome him to the family. It must have been in 1978 or 1979 – how old had she been? It was 1978. Her father, wearing a suit, carried her sister in his arms, and her mother, weeping, was in black. Her grandfather's first words were "A black dress? But we're not in mourning, daughter!" – and she doesn't even know if he embraced them. They had gone directly to Faliro, where a brand-new apartment with a sea view awaited him. He had finally decided to spend his last days in Greece. That was just the way it was, and he never discussed his decision. In front of her grandfather the sun sank behind the roofs of Mikrolimano, bristling with antennas.

Nikos and she ended up spending several days in her grandfather's place on Spetses. They slept in the bedroom where they used to come to spend weekends with Margarita. She couldn't stand the smell of the wardrobes, which would never lose the odour of the mothballs her grandfather had scattered in the drawers. Since her mother had considered it best to leave everything in the house as it was, each morning on her way downstairs she passed the pictures of mountain goats, pine trees and waterfalls that covered the walls. And Nikos? He ate in the kitchen with a hearty appetite and relaxed on the chaise longue, admiring the little bay and mocking her gently for a few days when she complained, "I can't stand those false paper flowers, or those lurid place mats."

It was then that Nikos uttered some words that put Christina beside herself: "You know, I'm feeling so marvellous, it's as if I'm in a family again at last." She had retorted, dryly, "Don't say that, do you hear? We're not a family; never say such a thing again!" For Christina, it was far too soon, for she was just getting to know Nikolaus Strom. He was her Nikos, her new love. But the mere word "family" reminded her of her failed marriage.

It was at that moment, as Christina is all too aware, that something had gone awry. Nikos hadn't replied, but she could see from his expression that she had hurt his feelings. She often thinks of that moment, like this morning after the phone call from the police. Christina no longer knows what the police represent. She doesn't even know any longer who controls what in the country. Soon she'll be in a car being driven to some place in Athens, then inside some office or other. Why can't they question her here? When they come for her, she'll offer them coffee.

Where will the car take her? To the police. She remembers that day on Alexandras Avenue with Nikos. It was spring, and they'd decided to go for lunch in a taverna in Exarcheia. As they sat in the car he gently made fun of her, laughing as he tried to change the station on the car radio, and she rapped him on the hand as soon as he turned the knob.

"Why do you always listen to Kosmos?" he asked. "They only play Latino music, and I'm here to listen to Greek songs."

All Athens was at their feet. Nikos had come for a few days, and Christina sensed that he was happy in the city, our city, of which she was part. She knew how much he identified her with the capital, the only place where she saw him really let himself go, in her arms, with a broad smile, like a child returning home after a long journey. She was driving along Alexandras Avenue; their hands had finally met on the car radio, and then the police pulled them over. They had to show their identity cards. There were three policemen, two of them riding motorcycles and masked beneath their helmets. Their eyes were unpleasant-looking; they walked slowly round the car, one hand on the butts of their revolvers. The one who had signalled to them to stop didn't say anything. They never discovered why the police were checking up on them.

Nikos was beside himself. "Do they think we're terrorists, or what? They're the terrorists, do you understand, Christina? Did you see the way they looked at us? Christina, say something! They didn't even give us an explanation."

She didn't really know what to think; she heard him talking about a dictatorship, the return of state violence, and Lord knows what else. She thought he was going too far, but she didn't dare say, "But you didn't live under the dictatorship, so what do you know about it?"

That morning, when she heard the man's voice on the phone, she told herself Nikos would have reacted badly, like that spring day on Alexandras Avenue.

Christina wonders, 'What have you done, my love, for this policeman to send for me?' She is sure it has something to do with his business. She'd warned him never to attempt to do business in Greece, and above all to have no dealings with the state. With every day that passes, she feels closer to him. She also knows that each new day returns them to the past. Lacking any future, their love is strengthened by the memory of what unites them forever. Nikos is hers forever, because he didn't know how. But for that he'd have needed to know he was. That day when she told him off so brutally for imagining they were a family together, why couldn't he have understood that that was what she wanted more than anything? Christina had realized it that day when they made love for the first time. For, after all, that evening, on the little square in

Kefalari, in front of the church, and later in the bar where they kissed like seventeen-year-olds, for, after all, when they made love for the first time in his room, for, after all, wasn't it then that they had defied distance for once and for all, denying the kilometres, denying anything that could separate them?

When he told her it was over, she could have remembered that, she should have taken out the little oval mirror she keeps in her handbag, held it up to him and asked him to repeat: It's over between us, over between us, over between us. Christina would like to throw it all in the face of the police, tell them all about it, get them to understand that Athens is no longer the same now that they're constantly patrolling the streets on their motorbikes. Not a single day without a police presence – a sign of weakness from a government of technocrats now obliged to defend itself against the people's wrath. Christina despises the stupidity of the police, their bullying blindness beneath their masks. She'll tell them how Nikos and she came together, he facing Mount Hymettus and she with her back against the chimney, completely exposed to the scorched flanks of Mount Pentelikon, in full sunlight, standing on the roof of her house, teetering in the heat of the day.

What did Nikos do, what did he do that they know about? Does she have to tell them all about him? She'll say he's innocent, that it's not his fault. It's just that he couldn't understand that you can only feel love once, forever, on a little square in Kefalari, in front of a little church, in the smell of the laurels that she remembers, and the smell of the pines through the windows open onto the streets of Melissia, making love at her place, in Athens, with a view of Mount Hymettus, of the sides of Mount Pentelikon, both of them panting on the roof, again, often at the height of midday, sometimes also motionless in front of a hearth in a taverna buried in the sand of Schinias, the long wintery beach, after an icy dip in the sea, both of them sitting in front of the fire licking their fingers dyed pink by the shrimps. The fire in the chimney, on their backs, but their love already dying out?

'Is it even possible for Athens to be just a brief passion snatched from the city's normal resistance?' In the evening, when the fragrance rises from the pine grove her balcony overlooks, Christina recalls, 'We've experienced it together, you and I, in the silence of nightfall, just before the crickets' chorus, when there was only the sound of our voices to convince us of our presence in the world.'

Nikos used to tell her that desire comes and goes, but she thought of it as something you enter and leave, like the tide ebbing and flowing on their beach at Schinias. She thought they spoke the same language, though she never told him so, never told him that they knew the source of the variance, and that the recurrence gave them pleasure. So why?

Today, she no longer recognizes anything: their café in Chalandri, the dry-cleaners in Melissia, the Cretan taverna in Kessariani, the Benaki Museum, the library on Stadiou, Doukissis Plakentias Metro station – it's as if the door of each was shut. The city is turning in on itself; her daughter asks her who are these people begging in front of her school gate, she finds people sleeping as if glued to the walls of the National Bank, she comes across students breaking pieces of marble from the Academy steps to use as ammunition; she sees more and more masked police, and Kosmos has stopped broadcasting music.

Christina doesn't know what nightmare her lover has ended up in, but maybe she's going to find out.

Her doorbell rings. The police have arrived. Christina goes out on the balcony and sees a face looking up at her.

"Mrs Lazaridou?"

"Yes, I'm coming, I'll be down right away."

It is a man with an inscrutable face; he is alone, in plain clothes, but he's a policeman all right, they just told her so, they'd warned her that she should be ready. She's coming, she'll be there directly.

Now the car is speeding towards Kifissia Avenue. Christina would like to open the window; she asks if she may and the man nods; he says nothing; he is driving very fast. That's odd, she thinks, he's turning right, towards Psychiko.

"Is this a shortcut?"

The policeman doesn't answer; the car bounces over a hump, but he doesn't slow down as he turns onto a little road that leads uphill. Halfway up, the car suddenly stops in front of the entrance to a little grey house surrounded by a neglected garden.

"Where are we?"

"We've arrived."

"But this isn't a police station; I was told it was the police. It's not the police?"

"If you like."

"But where are we? Who are you?"

The policeman has got out; he opens the car door and says, "This is an office of the Ministry of Public Order and Citizen Protection."

"I don't see any ministry here! Let me go, I refuse to set foot in that house, let me go, let me go, don't touch me, stop, do you hear, let me go!"

"Let her go!" says a man standing on the doorstep and holding the door open. The driver releases her arm. She can feel droplets of sweat running down her back, and doesn't budge from her seat. The man on the doorstep doesn't move; she can feel him looking her up and down and hears, "Mrs Lazaridou, please calm down! Follow me inside; nothing will happen to you."

"Yes, because I've my daughter; I must go and pick her up soon."

She enters the house, passing the man, who steps back to allow her through and smiles at her as she goes by; then she says to herself, 'Anyway, what choice do I have?'

She steps onto the marble floor of the little entrance hall and follows the man into a sparsely furnished room overlooking a bushy garden. She sits on a chair, and the man does likewise.

"Listen, Mrs Lazaridou, I did my best. It could have been worse."

"What you mean?"

"We could have sent uniformed police to fetch you. You know the kind of thing? They'd have knocked on your door and led you away like a vulgar criminal."

"I haven't done anything."

"A glass of water? Make yourself at home. You're welcome to smoke."

"I don't know what you want with me; I don't know anything."

"My name is Agent Evangelos, from the Ministry of Public Order and Citizen Protection, and as you know we have a few questions about Nikolaus Strom."

"Go on."

"First, are you aware of his whereabouts?"

"No, I know hardly anything about him, I haven't seen him for over a year. But why are the police looking for him?"

"When was your last contact with him exactly?"

"I don't know, three or four weeks ago; he called me at home to tell me he was going to the north of the country. But why —"

"We're the ones who ask the questions," interrupts Agent Evangelos. "But I should have started by asking you the nature of your relationship."

"What nature, what you mean? I don't understand your question."

"You and he —"

"We've gone our separate ways. For almost a year now. And anyway, what business is it of yours?"

"Nikos, is that what you call him?"

"Yes. Nikos, that's how he introduced himself to me. His mother is Greek, and he likes to be called Nikos."

"Tell me what you know about Nikolaus Strom, his profession, everything, everything."

"But you already know everything, don't you?"

"Listen, Mrs Lazaridou, it's in your best interest to cooperate with us. Nikolaus Strom is a murder suspect."

"Nikos, a murder suspect? That's impossible! He'd never kill anyone, I know him."

"Tell me everything you know about Nikolaus Strom. His age, his home address…"

"He was born in Hamburg, in 1971. He has an apartment there, I've forgotten the name of the street. He also has a studio apartment in Athens, on Rendi Street, in the Koukaki district, but it's been sublet for six months."

"And his profession?"

"Nikos is in business. He has his own company."

"What kind of business?"

"He sells security fences."

"What?"

"Well, fences! I don't know how to explain it to you."

"Please be more precise."

"He sells those barbed-wire fences, you know, like the ones between Mexico and the United States."

"Who are his customers for this material?"

"I really don't know. In his work, he always maintains contact with the army, with the frontier police."

"So it was in connection with his work that he came to Greece?"

"Initially, no. When I met him for the first time he was on holiday. He was trying to rediscover his Greek roots. He'd never spoken to me about his work. But one day he explained to me he was about to pull off a huge deal. He felt sure he'd be awarded the Greek contract of the century. That's when I found out what kind of business he was in. These past months, when I talked to him by phone, he said he was going to sell his fencing to the Greek government. It all began when he found out that Athens was prepared to pay three and a half million euros to build a wall along the Evros. Nikos said it was far too costly and that he could make a better offer."

"Do you know the name of Nikolaus Strom's company?"

"Security Fence Supplies, I think."

"Does he work alone? Have a secretary? An office in Greece?"

"No, he doesn't have any employees, and I'm not aware of any office in Greece."

"Where does he store his material?"

"He's never spoken to me about that kind of thing. He doesn't really like to talk about his work. All I know is that he collaborates a lot with an Israeli firm. I don't know what it's called, but it's they who deliver the material when Nikos has been awarded a contract. It's his first attempt to sell that filthy stuff here. I hate his job. And I always warned him never to work with Greece, because I was sure it would turn out badly."

"What you mean by that?"

"I knew he'd have problems if he did business with Greeks."

"And you're suggesting that he has had difficulties?"

"Yes."

"What kind of difficulties?"

"I don't have any details. But the last time we talked on the phone he mentioned some problems he was having with a colonel in the Greek army. This man was his contact for the sale of his damn barbed wire."

"Did he mention the colonel's name?"

"No, he didn't. He was calling me that day about something quite different. He wanted us to get together again. He was having second thoughts about our separation. It was only when I asked him what he was doing in northern Greece that he told me his business wasn't going the way he'd hoped. He was supposed to meet this colonel, but the man never turned up."

"And that's all he told you?"

"He also said he felt he was becoming paranoid. He thought he was being followed, but he wondered if maybe it was because our relationship was turning him crazy."

"I don't see the connection."

"I don't know. Nikos was very tense. He wasn't his usual self, and when I asked him what was going on he said, 'Nothing's going right for me: my business, the two of us, everything's going wrong. I'm miserable without you, and I'm afraid of something. And then I get the feeling that someone is following me. I feel I'm being watched everywhere I go.'"

Christina Lazaridou is free to go, but if she has to leave Athens she is requested to inform them. She finds the policeman with the inscrutable expression waiting in front of the house, but she would rather return to the avenue on foot and take a bus. She has told them everything she knows. The very notion that Nikos is a murderer is intolerable to her. But it's not her notion. She doesn't believe it for a moment. Christina suddenly remembers the day when she'd booked a table in a restaurant overlooking the Mesogaia plain. Nikos had liked the view, saying that from the spot where they sat, on a terrace overlooking the plain, the aeroplanes looked like toys and the runway quivering in the sunlight was like a mirage. Nikos had said that the entire parched landscape, the control tower, and the planes landing and taking off, were all just an illusion, and that it really proved there was no distance between them. He was happy, and the holiday could begin with this vibrant image of time suddenly arrested in the violent shimmering of the tarmac.

When she smokes on her balcony Christina often thinks of Athens airport, she imagines it as a model set down on the red soil of Attica, on this bare landscape devoid of shade, under the unwavering sun. There, everything is just a treasure hunt, comings and goings, losses, reunions, all just provisional, surface movements, kite flyers on a very windy afternoon.

Agent Evangelos is standing by the window. In the garden of the little house used by the National Intelligence Service the last rays of sunlight filter through the dry leaves of a neglected clump of laurels. Inside the room the evening light plays with the outsized shadow of the single chair where, barely an hour ago, Nikolaus Strom's ex-girlfriend was sitting. Nikolaus Strom, a German with a Greek mother, born in Hamburg in 1971, hoping to win the contract for the wall on the Greco-Turkish frontier. Evangelos looks in his jacket pocket for his cigarettes. He knows he won't find any, but the gesture, the mere action of looking for them, is something at least, and then – why not? – he should have asked the Lazaridou woman for one or two. A very attractive woman, he thinks.

He'll have to take a closer look at those kilometres of barbed wire that the Greek government wants to roll out between Greece and Turkey. A rampart against migrants with an estimated cost of three and a half million euros. 'A lot of money for a damn fence,' thinks Evangelos. 'And Athens wants Brussels to fork out the cash. Well, that's understandable, since it's also the European Union's frontier.'

Now the thing is to get hold of this Nikolaus Strom as soon as possible. 'Nikos, as his lady friend calls him.' Agent Evangelos smiles, thinking back. 'And closing the case is out of the question. My directorate will get quite a jolt when they learn that the suspect in the Evros murder case was trying to sell a barbed-wire wall to the Greek army.'

Outside, darkness has enveloped the deserted garden. Behind Agent Evangelos someone has opened the door and he can feel the draught accompanying the unfriendly presence of the driver, who is watching him call headquarters on his mobile. Buzzing gently, a distraught fly circles the ceiling light, which flashes intermittently. Without turning around, but looking up at the insect, Evangelos says, "You can go, I don't need you any more. I'm going to stay on for a while, and I've got a phone call to make, as you can see." He hears the front door close, rattling the glass panel. He opens the window and switches off the light. He only gets a continuous ring tone from the other end. The fly has finally settled. From outside comes the sound of a departing vehicle.

'That driver, what a moron,' thinks Agent Evangelos. 'He reminds me of those hatchet men under the dictatorship.'

"Hello?"

"Ah, about time! I have some news —"

"So have we, Agent Evangelos; there's been a missing person reported in the Evros region."

"Who?"

"Batsis, Andreas Batsis. He may well be your headless corpse."

"*Our* corpse, you mean! Did his family call to say they hadn't heard from him?"

"No, there's no family, no use looking in that direction."

"I don't understand."

"All you need to do is check his DNA with the forensic pathologist in Alexandroupolis. We just have to make sure that the dead man is really Batsis, and then leave everything just the way it is – and make sure this business doesn't get out."

"If you say so. But now listen to me, I have some information."

"You're talking about Strom?"

"Yes. He runs a company that sells security fences. He was hoping to sell us his material to build the wall."

"We know all about that."

"What? But who told you?"

"Don't ask pointless questions, Agent Evangelos!"

"Oh, come on, what kind of game are you playing with me? Are you also aware that he was in contact with an army colonel?"

"We know all about that. Just forget about it. The important thing now is to get our hands on Strom. But be careful, he's no longer wanted for murder. You understand, he's no longer wanted for murder!"

"What?"

"Strom is guilty of illegally entering a military zone. That's the only thing of interest to us. Do you understand what I'm saying?"

"For God's sake —"

"Agent Evangelos! Not for murder. We are trying to get our hands on a German national who ignored the perfectly visible signs identifying a military zone situated on our strategic frontier with Turkey. We have to catch this individual immediately. There's not a moment to lose!"

"What is this crap?"

"Evangelos, just do what you're asked."

"What about the minister? Does he know?"

"Don't worry about that, the minister has enough on his plate with Berlin and the Troika."

"Oh, go to hell!"

"Don't swear like that, Agent Evangelos. Forget this decapitation business once for all. Just verify Batsis's DNA."

Agent Evangelos hangs up. A gust of humid air enters the room, along with the cool smell of the pines. Standing in front of the window, he reviews everything he knows.

'Someone has decapitated a man possibly named Batsis, a person known to the security services. Anyway, that's the version provided by a Russian escort, Polina Zubov, who ran away from a brothel called the Eros, the scene of the crime, less than three kilometres from the Turkish border. This individual, the prime suspect for this murder by decapitation, is named Nikolaus Strom. A German national, of Greek origin on his mother's side, he apparently owns a small company specializing in the sale of security fences. According to his former lady friend, Christina Lazaridou, a resident of Athens, Strom was visiting the Evros region in his attempt to win a large contract, namely for the construction of a twelve-and-a-half-kilometre barbed-wire barrier on the Greco-Turkish frontier – a fence which the Greek government hopes will put an end to illegal migrants crossing onto its territory. It seems that Strom was in touch with a colonel in the Greek army.'

Once again, Agent Evangelos searches through his pockets for his cigarettes, an old reflex that returns when he is under stress. 'So far it all seems pretty clear,' he tells himself. 'The bits of the puzzle fit together perfectly. But then why is the directorate asking me to drop the murder charge? Who is this Batsis, whose horrible death doesn't seem to bother anyone? The victim is known to our services... so...?

'The most surprising thing,' Agent Evangelos tells himself, 'is this business about the military zone. It's true, Strom was wrong to go wandering along the banks of that damned river Evros. A fat lot of good it did him anyway. But why is the entire Greek police hunting for him because he has set foot on that blasted no man's land when he's really the prime suspect in the murder of a Greek citizen?'

Agent Evangelos isn't going to let the matter drop. 'I'll get hold of this Strom, and worm out of him whether he was really the one who decapitated that individual on the banks of the Evros. It's purely for my own interest, because I want to discover that tiny fragment of the truth; a truth being treated as that insignificant must be upsetting for a lot of people. After that, we'll see what the directorate wants.'

It is almost eleven. Evangelos must phone his daughter. This will be a special Christmas: his first Christmas as a grandfather. He'll call his daughter, and then… No, first he'll call Lieutenant Anastasis and tell him he'll be back in the Evros region tomorrow, he'll tell him they'll spend the holiday together touring the zone along the river in his jeep. 'But no,' decides Agent Evangelos. 'First I have to eat something. But not just anywhere.'

Agent Evangelos knows where to find Sokratis Retzeptis. At this late hour, Christmas celebrations or no, street demonstrations or no, his old friend generally takes refuge in a tavern on Mavromichali Street, in Pinaleon. Sokratis used to be a judge in the Athens Court of Appeal, and his close links with the political class have often overstepped the strict boundaries of judicial independence. Evangelos has never known whose side Sokratis is really on. But he is sure of one thing: Sokratis has never done anything damaging to him, Agent Evangelos, and his advice has always proved valuable. When he was twenty, in 1974, Sokratis fell madly in love with a dark-haired young girl who wore her hair very short, in defiance of her family. One evening in August, on the way to Sounion, at the Varkiza crossroads, a car cut off Sokratis's motorbike. He got off with lying immobilized in a hospital bed for six months. His passenger with the tomboy haircut wasn't wearing a helmet. She died on the spot. She was eighteen; her name was Fotini, and she was Agent Evangelos's sister. 'She was my little sister.'

Evangelos has arrived in front of a house straight from the time when shepherds grazed their sheep on rocky Mount Lycabettos. He picks his way along a narrow corridor cluttered with a pile of large fig-tree logs and enters a room resembling the storeroom of some eccentric second-hand dealer.

Sokratis is there, surrounded by his usual band of comrades from PASOK. No ministers or civil servants, just 1974 intellectuals, as Evangelos calls them, men of his generation, born in the 1940s and 1950s: university professors, journalists, architects – his contemporaries, men who aren't deceived by the great shadow play being acted out in Greece. They are corrupt to varying degrees, more or less fortunate scions suckled at the breast of the state, but not yet infected by the terrible disgrace which little by little is dulling our gaze.

This evening, as always, the familiar smell of cooking, the twanging of the *baglamas* and the smoke of cigarettes that they persist in smoking indoors in futile revolt against the diktats from Brussels, succeed in dissipating a vague sense of guilt, for outside, down in the streets of Exarcheia, devastated a few hours before by yet another riot, Agent Evangelos had told himself, 'Our children are hurting themselves.'

"Our children are hurting themselves," Agent Evangelos shouts to make himself heard, resting a hand on the shoulder of Sokratis, who smiles back at him from a murky mirror.

"You're right," yells Sokratis. "It's as if they were cutting themselves, like kids punishing themselves for the suffering inflicted by their parents. But sit down, and don't cry, Evangelos!"

"I'm not crying, it's the tear gas, foul stuff! Hours after the demonstration it's still lingering in the streets nearby."

"You're right to say they're only hurting themselves."

Around the table, the conversation is becoming heated. Mouths open and shut like clappers in faces too fleshy or too bony; moustaches quiver, bald pates glow like light bulbs.

"Yes, it's true! Why don't they set fire to Kifissia? Talk about a revolution! They're destroying for the sake of destruction, smashing bus shelters, little stores; hooligans, the lot of them."

Sokratis leans towards Agent Evangelos. "You haven't come to see me to express your astonishment at the sight of our children destroying their own neighbourhood instead of taking it out on the wealthy suburbs where we all live, we, their unworthy parents. Why are you here, for God's sake?"

"Because I'm hungry and thirsty, and I'm travelling

tomorrow," replies Agent Evangelos, ordering a plate of beef and vegetable soup.

"You're wise to eat something, my old friend, you're not looking so great. Worries?"

"No, it's because I'm a grandfather now. It ages me!"

"Andromeda had her baby? Boss, a jug of raki here! Evangelos is a grandfather! It's a boy?"

"A girl."

"Never mind, that's good too!"

Agent Evangelos is a grandfather, and the others call out, "So you're a granddad?" And he repeats, "Yes, I'm a granddad!" And he tells himself it's time he retired, but he's not going to come drinking raki every evening with Sokratis and his gang, he'd rather go to his own bar, the Batman. On his own, the way he likes to go jogging on the flanks of Mount Hymettus, around the monastery, where there was the big fire in the summer of 2007.

Sokratis lays his hand on Agent Evangelos's arm, squeezes it hard, and says, "Now tell me what has brought you into my den on Christmas Eve, tell me what brought you here, for God's sake, you know how impatient I am!"

Agent Evangelos smiles at his old friend, looking him straight in the eye, and when Sokratis finally lowers his gaze, he whispers in his ear, "The wall!"

"What about the wall?"

"That's what I'd like you to find out for me: about the wall, you know, the wall!"

"No, I've no idea what you're talking about!"

"Don't take me for a fool. It's the only thing that matters to the higher-ups right now. The wall."

"What do you need to know?"

"I need to know who was awarded the contract to build the wall."

"Now, there you go, suddenly spoiling my dinner! You're asking too much."

"Find out for me!"

"But you're the one who works for our National Intelligence Service, aren't you?"

"Yes, and that's exactly why I don't know who I can ask to get the right answers."

"I'll look into it tomorrow."

"Thanks, and let the phone ring, don't worry if I don't pick it up right away. Where I'll be, up north, the network doesn't always work too well."

"You're off to do some hunting, then?"

"Yes, along the Evros."

"Take care, then; it's a nature reserve, with protected species."

"I know! The bird I'm after has the advantage of some very special cover. He's a killer, yet the directorate wants him arrested for something else."

"Now you're talking in riddles!"

"You've trained me well, haven't you?"

Agent Evangelos swallows his raki in a single gulp, gets up, and says goodbye all around. His old friend holds his jacket for him.

"Evangelos, take care you don't come a cropper."

"What are you trying to tell me?"

"Take care not to come a cropper against that wall. It would be too stupid. You're a granddad now."

Episode V

Nikolaus Strom sometimes feels that everything is within: the lantern suspended from the ceiling, creaking in the icy wind, his shadow shifting to and fro on the parapet, and the snowflakes drifting down in front of the walls of the old Koranic school.

Snow is lying on the quay where the ferries dock. From above, he can see the dark tracks left by two police cars. He senses that they will return, yet he doesn't take cover in the inside courtyard of the luxury hotel. Until this evening he had thought no one would come looking for him here. He has restored his energy in the Imaret Hotel, whose majestic shape dominates the harbour of Kavala. But the nightmare still haunts him. Reclining on the wide bed strewn with kilim cushions, he has revisited everything that occurred in the unre-membering space of the river. Earlier that afternoon he had barely closed his eyes in the scalding hot bath when he had the vision of the man's face. But he can't recall anything more; the same dark scene is repeated, nothing more.

'When did it all begin?' he wonders. When did his world begin to fall apart? For a few days now, he has felt as if borne along on a dark, tumultuous current. And then there's Christina. He tells himself he must stop thinking about her. He must abandon everything and escape from Greece as quickly as possible.

The last ferry of the year should have sailed by now. But the door of the ship's hold is closed only halfway. Two large forklift trucks are blocking the loading ramp. The Thassos Express won't be putting to sea this evening, and it has nothing to do with the bad weather or the New Year celebrations.

A hubbub suddenly rises from the port, a din of horns, voices, with blue revolving lights flashing on the white hull of the ferry.

The snow is still falling. He still doesn't understand what is happening to him. He tells himself there must be an explanation. He reassures himself with the idea that the police aren't there because of him, but to breach the picket lines of the striking dockers.

'How did I get mixed up in all this?' he wonders. He still can't understand how it all went wrong. There are police everywhere. When he came ashore from the Samothrace ferry around ten o'clock, shortly before the dockers' strike began, he understood why he felt afraid on noticing those two men. What if they were looking for him as he disembarked? He had seen them, and told himself, 'It's for me, it's the police. Maybe they've arrested the girl? Maybe she's talked?' He wonders why she didn't wait for him. She was gone. He had told her to wait for him. And what if she'd blamed him for killing that man? No, that wasn't possible.

Nikolaus was still on the deck when he felt the panic rising. He had just noticed the two men and seen them scrutinizing the faces of all the passengers as they disembarked. He didn't know if they were police or the other ones, the ones he has never seen but whose presence he has sensed over the past few weeks.

Someone was following him, spying on him. Until the evening when the meeting was supposed to take place in that damned brothel, he had thought that his life was following a rational pattern. 'My name is Nikolaus Strom, but I prefer to be called Nikos. That's what Christina calls me, "Nikos, my Nikos," she'd say, for it's all over between us now, and that's the way it had to be. My name is Nikos; I left Christina and travelled to the Evros region on business. I was offering them a wall for half the cost: two rows of barbed wire, identical to the set-up proposed by the government but for half the cost.'

That was how things stood, Nikos saw it clearly, he accepted it. But everything had gone wrong. The first alarm coincided with his arrival in Alexandroupolis. Everywhere he went, someone was watching him, like when he was waiting for the Greek army colonel supposed to drive him again over the twelve and a half kilometres of the floodplain along which the fence is to be erected. The time they made their initial survey of the area he had felt he could trust the colonel, but then the man failed to turn up for their second rendezvous. Nikos sensed at the time that he wasn't alone in that restaurant on the port where they had arranged to meet. He knew very well that the waitress and he were alone in the place, but when he thought back on it he was ready to swear he was being watched. He waited, consulted his watch, and wondered, 'Why is the colonel so late?' The hours went by, but still no one came. The waitress yawned; Nikos consulted his mobile: no call, nothing apart from his feeling of being watched. And then everything went haywire.

It really was the police waiting at the exit from the ferry that morning. But they weren't there on his account. They were in plain clothes, looking for that poor lad he'd seen on the dock in Alexandroupolis: a youngster, no more than a teenager, a migrant, one among the hundreds every year who try to leave Thrace, reach Thessalonica, and then travel on to Athens. Like Nikolaus, the boy had told himself that the railway station wasn't safe because of the ticket inspections. Like Nikolaus, he had taken the ferry to the island of Samothrace. They had both waited a day before taking another ferry to Kavala, covering their tracks and already a little farther along their way, not taking the train and avoiding the roads, which were all too closely watched.

Nikos had been hoping to sell his wall to Greece, but now he talks about it in the past tense. Now everything has changed. He should have listened to Christina; the match was too unequal. His competition was too powerful. He must have greased a few palms. Otherwise, how could it be explained that Nikos's offer, the offer made by Nikolaus Strom, his offer, wasn't accepted? 'Half the cost, my wall! Why did the army and the frontier people take me for a ride like that?' All his contacts, like Colonel Papadopoulos, had dropped him. When you consider that he was offering them a wall identical with his competitor's – but at half the cost... And then there's the political context: the German government is opposed to the wall, and Brussels doesn't want to pay for it. But that has nothing to do with Nikos. And in any case the colonel had arranged to meet him in that brothel on the frontier. He'd told him that it was an ideal spot to talk "business". It was an ambush, he sees that now, a trap he fell into blindly.

On the port, three more police cars arrive as reinforcements. From the terrace of the Imaret Nikos can make out men in fatigues boarding the ship, climbing rope ladders they have thrown up. He has seen enough. It's time he took refuge inside the hotel. In the courtyard, all is quiet. The water has frozen in the big blue pool. A warm light is flickering behind the window of his room. Room service has lit a fire in the grate. He undresses. His bare feet sink into a thick woollen carpet. Crouching in front of the fireplace, he looks for the little carafe of raki offered as a welcome gift. He drinks it slowly, sinking into a gentle torpor. He would like to think of Christina, but already the vision of the head reappears. This time it falls off and rolls into a ditch. He drives the nightmare away, thinking of Crete, of that summer when they took the boat to Chania and Christina was so happy.

The scene is repeated; the pink lettering of the brothel's neon sign hurts his eyes. He can hear the girl's yells; she has Christina's face. He wakes in a sweat, wanting to vomit.

The precise image of the head falling off finally disappears, as the body did. Why did nothing remain but the head? The girl was shaking all over; she spoke to him in Russian. He shivers. The fire in the grate has gone out. He looks for the central-heating remote, without success. He returns to bed and buries himself beneath the covers. The years he spent with Christina are behind him now. Yesterday evening, on his own, as he watched the snow falling in the Imaret's inner courtyard, he struggled against the memory of that spring when, as a surprise for him, she had reserved a room in Ali Pasha's former seigneurial residence. "I was sure you'd like it," she'd said. "You know, this residence was built in 1817 by the founder of modern Egypt. But wait, you haven't seen the bathroom yet!"

A magnificent Ottoman palace, one of the few still existing in Greece, a gift from Christina on the anniversary of their meeting on Eleni's balcony in Pieraki. Memories of Christina, a rising tide, a dangerous undertow, the steaming bathwater, all the rooms of the Imaret open to her: she had the run of the place. But yesterday, to drive away the memory of that head, he had remained outside, watching the snow fall among the marble columns of the former madrasa.

Don't turn around, leave as fast as his legs can carry him. Concentrate on the carols broadcast by the loudspeakers in the courtyard: "Jingle Bells", "O Holy Night". The seasons pass. It's been a summer, a winter, a new year since they parted ways: the Christmas music underscores the distance. But there's nothing to measure the distance of time's passing since that summer day when he was heading along Kolokotroni Street, in Kifissia. Christina was waiting for him as he tried to find the location of their first rendezvous. She was there: hadn't she said she would be? Then his dawning smile of gratitude to let her know – at this spot, the square in Kefalari, rendezvous at 9.30 in front of the church, yes, that's the place – she should know that this was where he began a new life. Christina in white, her cheek offered to his still non-lover's kiss, her cheeks, kisses, one on each, and off they go, walking now, he searching for a bench, two people already in love, and knowing it, but looking for a bar as if nothing out of the ordinary had occurred, still pretending.

Christina and he discovering one another, their hands, then their knees, their tongues, in unison, exploring. What took place between them is almost a journey. Christina and he are seen on the Athenian plain; they are leaving the heights of Kifissia by car; driving through a residential neighbourhood, stepwise along one, then two, then three tree-lined avenues connected by little one-way streets that intersect them at right angles. She is driving, at the wheel of her blue Citroën Picasso, a rather dilapidated family car, with a child seat in the back. Nikolaus sees himself sitting in the car; he knows he is there, just as he is aware that what is happening at that moment involves traffic, is inscribed on a map of the city: a roundabout, followed by a small bridge, passing abandoned buildings that stand in an expanse of dry grass, glimpsing the vestiges of a pine forest on the slopes of Mount Pentelikon, the mountain with a bald summit that had so often burned, and halfway up, which you have to drive around to reach Melissia, once nothing but beehives but now all five-storey apartment buildings replete with flower-decked balconies and brightly coloured awnings.

Their route, that first time, took them past the tavern on the corner of a square in the centre of which the church faced them that night, as it would on every subsequent occasion; Christina and he driving along a cobbled road that led off behind the brick church, their momentum hindered by the raised railway crossing. Then a stop sign she ignored without a smile, both hands on the wheel, seeming to obey something beyond them both but more perceptible to the driver, obliged to admit that she was powerless to do anything about it.

The Picasso climbs ever more narrow streets lined with cars whose bodywork shines like the dark waters of a moonlit bay. He can still see himself: it is really he, sitting beside Christina, her passenger, transported into a new geography of Athens that arouses him.

They have arrived. Christina reaches through the Picasso's window to point the remote at the gate. This wasn't the first time he had met her. He still wonders if Christina got out of the car. She must have walked towards the door of her building, and he must have followed her.

And he, getting out in turn, locked to her, to the rough swish of her rope soles, following the resolute advance of her sandals, from that moment, and for some time, forever, as you must believe at such moments, in Christina's footsteps, feeling his way on the steep flank of Mount

Pentelikon that surrounds her, at her pace, in the rush of his blood, swelling, towed in her wake, dragged along, until the final hollow before the hump where, it is said, fate goes awry: actually just the building and its driveway, the little garden, the intermittent jet of the sprinkler, a ball, more cars, but they belong to the neighbours, the glow of spotlights among the laurels, crickets chirping, the friction of the door against on the hall mat, a marble table, envelopes on the floor, floodlighting, a lift, staircases, a door on the first floor, the sound of a key in the lock, a new fragrance: Christina, he entering her flat. The entrance through the living room. The sandals again, the corridor, the bedroom, an unfamiliar laundry smell, her personal chemistry. The sound of the switch, too much light, maybe turn it off?

"Well, I mean, can't we turn it off?"

The night light on the bedside table, a neatly made bed, dark sheets, Christina standing on one leg, and as her arm seems to go looking for the other one bent behind her back, a sudden right angle, the weight of her foot in the air – at that moment Christina only had her sandals left as, balanced on one leg with her ankle folded back behind her buttocks, she tries to reach the little tongue in the buckle, and that is when he moves forward and says no, he'd like to do it with the rope soles on, would that be all right?

A terrace, that was immediately after, but it will always remain with him. She led him outside, that night, as she always would. Behind the pine forest the winking summit of Mount Hymettus was visible. Later, a dog would bark.

Then that feeling of having arrived somewhere – in other words, of being finally *there*, of a homecoming.

A ship's siren. But that was not what made him open his eyes. The siren had emitted several blasts, and he had let it penetrate his sleep. No, in his room in the Imaret Nikolaus is awakened by something else. He has heard voices in the inner courtyard. A pale light filters through the half-open window. It is barely dawn. Nikolaus leaps out of bed and, without showing himself, looks outside. It's the police. He can see two uniformed men talking to the receptionist, and another, in plain clothes, on the wooden gallery overlooking the courtyard. Nikolaus dresses quickly and presses his ear to the door. Now the voices are distinct. The police are asking to search the entire hotel, they're looking for a "terrorist, a spy", a dangerous individual. The receptionist asks them to wait; he protests. Voices are raised, and then he hears his name: Strom.

"At least wait until I call the management," says the receptionist.

"That's not possible. We'll assemble everyone here in the courtyard," replies a policeman, the one in plain clothes, who has just joined his colleagues.

"Have you seen the time? You'll frighten our guests. Since you're here, why not wait for my boss. If your fugitive is hiding somewhere in the hotel, he has no way to escape."

"Stop arguing! And lower your voice. We're counting on the element of surprise. Go and fetch me the list of your guests instead."

Nikos can feel his heart beating very fast. He needs air. He takes two steps and leans against the wall. He keeps quite still, breathing through his mouth, as if he lacks oxygen. He recovers his breath, immediately pulls on his jacket and hat, throws his things into his bag, and makes for the back of the room where a large antique buffet conceals half of an ancient sealed-up door. During his first day at the Imaret with Christina he had taken great interest in the architecture of this former Koranic school now converted into a hotel, and had discovered that some of the rooms, like the one he occupies, open onto another courtyard, now closed to the public, which is lined with ancient prayer cells used by the cleaning staff for storage. One of the cells, as he remembers from the tour of the premises he made, opens onto a rooftop catwalk from where there are stairs leading down to an alleyway in the old town. With a single blow from his shoulder, Nikos cracks open the wooden door, whose worm-eaten boards yield easily. The pale light of early dawn enters through the gap. His escape route leads ahead, through the radiant silence of the empty courtyard. He glances right and left. No one in sight. Not one footstep in the fresh snow. He steps outside. The sky has emerged cloudless from the night, but he still hesitates in the shadow of the old walls with their broken-down balconies. Nikos locates the cell that opens onto the catwalk, and heads directly for it. Fortunately, it is not locked. Inside, he hurries to a narrow window, passes his bag through it, and wriggles after it. A few steps along the catwalk and he reaches the stairs, which are closed off by a little gate he can easily step over and descend to the snow-covered cobblestones of the alleyway. There is still no one in sight. Nikos can see the hills above the roofs of the old town of Kavala. If he can reach them he'll have escaped the police. Now he must walk, not thinking about the footprints left behind him. His pursuers will be able to follow this trail for barely a hundred metres, and then the trace of his soles will have been absorbed in the mud of the already sunlit street corner. Avoiding haste, not to arouse suspicion, he comes to a little square. Still no one, he tells himself. But three men appear. They pass in front of him, and suddenly the sound bursts out in the air, like the ripe pomegranates smashed on Greek doorsteps to mark the New Year. They are musicians. The first, a stout man with a moustache, plays the big drum; it is he who strikes up the march. The eldest member of the little band, grey-haired and as skinny as a dead tree branch, follows him playing a *gaida* while a youngster too lightly dressed for the season brings up the rear, blowing into a trumpet with all his might. The numbers of this little group grow at each street corner as other members of the procession join in, and no one seems surprised to see a stranger join the joyful troop to celebrate the New Year.

With his hat pulled down over his face, Nikos doesn't bother to lower his head when police cars pass, not even slowing as they draw level with the procession. A little girl plays the triangle; her mother distributes treats. Fritters pass from hand to hand. He is offered a piece of pitta, and bites into it. As the drum echoes throughout the town he feels something hard under a tooth: a bean.

*

Nikos asks his way. The people he consults point towards the white heights of Kavala.

"The Egnatia Odos? Up that way."

"The motorway? Too far, you can get there by bus, take a No. 1."

"The A2? It's that way, just turn up Egnatia Street, you can't miss it. But you're not driving?"

He sets off on foot, climbing the riverbed of Kavala's steep streets, stepping over rivulets of red earth, often changing sides, even venturing along the pavement booby-trapped by the National Electricity Company, which has grown weary of refilling the holes. Behind the fugitive's footsteps the town sinks back like a sandcastle collapsing on a shoreline battered by the compact mass of the sea and tinted red by erosion from the hills. Far behind – but he won't turn around – lie the tiled roofs of a town directly in line with an Ottoman aqueduct, some houses built into a wall, and, towering over the port, the domes of the Imaret. Along the seashore, the snow has melted. The police must be all over the town by now. A while ago he could hear the scream of sirens in the suburbs.

He has no choice. He must get to Bulgaria. He had sensed that in Greece he had become a bother to some-one, and now he's on the run. Directly ahead is the road, the Egnatia Odos, high up behind the pine forest where the snow is still lying. Head east, on foot all the way to the Bulgarian border, and then we'll see. Meanwhile, never look back. The police think he's an accessory to murder. And maybe they think he's the killer. Forget the head falling, the girl's screams. That head… he'd seen it somewhere before. When it parted from the man's body, as he was dragging the body and suddenly the head parted from it, he had told himself he'd seen that face somewhere before. Probably one of the men who was watching him, one of the colonel's men. The more he thinks about it the more he is convinced it wasn't the girl the man was after, but him, Nikos. The rendezvous at the Eros was a trap, now he is sure of it.

He keeps going; he is on the run, trying to find his way. "The Egnatia Odos, you're looking for the E90?" The young man in the shop where he bought water and provisions stares at him, astonished. "Two kilometres ahead. You can't miss it."

He walks between gutted houses, still asking his way but not listening to the directions: he only asks so that he can hear his own voice, as if to convince himself of his unmerited punishment, the loss of Christina and the business of the head. With his rucksack, bulky jacket and woollen hat, he goes from hill to hill on the frosty heights above Kavala, never looking back, searching for an ancient road marked out by milestones. It's not the modern road to Turkey he's looking for, not the trans-European motorway with its covered lorries that negotiate the turns at reduced speed, throwing up meltwater with the roar of a mountain stream.

Now Nikos is making his way along a hillside, the first part of his route already traced on the damp, mossy path. He walks with high, resolute steps, indifferent to his sole companion – a salty wind that chases through the pines and is now about to obliterate his footprints on the heights above Kavala. In a spot called Vyronas the ancient road appeared. The snow, which still lies on the olive branches on either side of the path, hasn't survived on the first step along the granite paving stones. As he sets foot on them he feels a kind of warmth pass beneath his soles. Now something leads onward: maybe his way beginning at last. On this new prominence, he suddenly perceives the present with greater assurance – the assurance of advancing step by step. For if his eyes think they must avoid the brittle bouquet of a dead tree, if his arms still ache from lifting lattices of fragile branches, or if his ears persist in hearing a crow's alarm cry in a copse, his feet are treading the Egnatia Odos with no more obstacles to overcome, surrounded by things, in the clarity of flight. On his way – and it's no longer an image – with nowhere to call home, he is making his escape. And after walking for three good hours, he has looked up from the ground. Now the Egnatia Odos is no more than a direction, for the paved road has not withstood the erosion of centuries. On the narrow pass across Mount Symbolon the snow is more stubborn. But the dense, rolling fog, penetrated by sunlight, is lifting over the olive groves that cling to the steep slopes of the steaming mountain. On its crest, by noon the entire landscape will be flowing down into the Drama plain. It will be time to make a halt, and draw breath. But there is no dry stone to sit on, no shelter, just the feel of his overheated limbs and the protective cover of his woollen hat gleaming with dew.

The sun has disappeared. Nikos is following a sheep track. In his flight, he has been walking for hours, but all that matters right now is his perception of a circular space around his advancing body. He knows this light well, its comforting pallor. It took winter in Thessalonica for him to notice it for the first time. It was one evening in February, when he disembarked at Macedonia Airport. Flying out of Hamburg, he had taken off from Vienna two hours earlier, dazzled through the aeroplane window by the broad mirror of the river. The Danube plains were sparkling in the setting sun, so when the first pilot announced the ground temperature at their destina- tion – minus two Celsius – he wasn't sure he had heard correctly. A glance at the limestone terrain, barely veiled in mist, gave no hint of the snowstorm descending onto the Balkans from Russia. The meteorologists had got it right, for approaching Belgrade the plane plunged into in a profound, whistling darkness.

The descent over Bulgaria was accompanied by strong turbulence, and when they reached the Thermaic Gulf the silence in the cabin deepened as the blizzard clawed at the plane's hull. Then nothing but clouds, and the landing.

The plane left three dark tracks in the layer of pow- dery snow on the tarmac. Already standing up, defying instructions, the tired-looking passengers were donning capes and woollen overcoats. Nikos had remained in his seat, forehead pressed to the glass. As his eyes tried to follow the flakes whirling in the beam of a large spot- light that was pointed at the arrival area, it occurred to him that he would remain here longer than he had planned. Something – he didn't know what – was pulsing within him.

In the bus with its wet, salt-stained floor, he caught himself smiling at his blurred reflection in the fogged-up window. When he reached the luggage carousel, where the passengers formed a dark, compact hedge, like mourners watching a coffin being borne from a church, he was again overcome by this feeling to which he found it difficult to put a name.

He had been waiting for half an hour in the freezing arrivals hall when he suddenly become aware that everyone had left yet there was still no sign of his suitcase. An airport employee, who had added a scarf and gloves to his thin uniform, emerged from nowhere and addressed him in Greek, asking: "Which flight did you come off, sir?"

"From Vienna," he'd answered in his mother tongue, which he hadn't spoken for some time.

"Then you're at the wrong carousel. That one was for the plane from Athens. Austrian is at number three, behind you."

He turned around and saw his suitcase, finely coated with snow, circulating on the carousel under the soft-olive neon light. It was then that he understood what had been animating him since his arrival in Thessalonica: an immense joy.

Nikos stopped thinking. Now he has left behind the frozen heights of Mount Pangaion, which bars the access to the Aegean, and is advancing across the Lekani range. He could have followed the coast from Kavala and then hugged the E90, passing under the monumental arches of the motorway bridges, and gone around the southern side of the mountain. He could equally well have rented a car from one of those agencies with their garish signs, taking the keys to a metallic-green Nissan that, as usual, blocks the pavement in front of the car rental agencies in Greece, and steered with one hand through the depressing suburbs surrounding the port. He had been too hasty, he shouldn't have given in to panic, even at the risk of being spotted by the police, who must have erected roadblocks. Didn't he leave his mobile in the hotel room? For Nikos, everything is clear: the police are on his heels. They are moving heaven and earth to catch the individual who chopped off a man's head outside that brothel. And – he still finds it difficult to believe – that individual is he!

Nikos doesn't have time to pursue these reflections. Even before he hears it, he sees the danger that suddenly emerges ahead. It skims the crest of the mountain before plunging into the valley he is in: a helicopter. Without a moment's hesitation Nikos takes cover; he crawls towards a bank, and slides down the remaining snow on his stomach. The clatter of the rotors explodes above him; in a fraction of a second he sees the aircraft's white underbelly passing overhead. Nikos makes for a rock against which he huddles, camouflaging himself with a pile of damp leaves. The engine's racket moves away. From where he is, he has a view over the forest and can make out a road, carved out of the rock below. The helicopter hovers at the entrance to a little tunnel, mere metres above the ribbon of asphalt. It finally comes to rest in the middle of the road, its engine still running. Four men in military fatigues jump out and set off to explore the tunnel. About twenty minutes later the helicopter takes off in a northerly direction. Nikos resumes his progress, careful never to leave the cover of the trees. In the afternoon, dog-tired, he finds himself facing a pyramid-shaped mountain at the entrance to a little combe with a stream running through it. Looking up, he can see a roof that draws a grey streak across a bright patch of meadow. He estimates at a glance that it will take him at least two hours to reach this refuge – and that's discounting the snow which is beginning to fall in tiny flakes. In no time at all the sky darkens and a storm comes up. No longer able to tell if he is heading in the right direction, Nikos tries to follow a path which had seemed to lead to the meadow. Frozen stiff, his face lashed by the gusting wind, he has left the trees half an hour behind when he bumps into a wooden fence. The sheepfold is very close; he can make out its elongated shape, and reaches it after crossing a field blanketed in a thick layer of fresh snow. Bowing his head under the eaves, he pushes open the door of the drystone building. He brushes off his jacket which bristles with tiny snow crystals, stamps his feet as he would have done out of consideration when entering someone's home, and slips inside. His feet encounter a floor of beaten earth, as soft as a carpet. His knee strikes something solid, which makes a sharp sound as it falls. His eyes become accustomed to the dark. He had knocked over a chair with a straw seat; he picks it up and collapses onto it.

Everything is silent. The sheepfold is empty, and the cold has obliterated even the animals' smell. There remains only a vague odour of oil, like lamp oil. He finally makes out a table, one leg of which he can touch with the toe of his boot. He gets to his feet and slowly brushes off its icy surface with one hand. It encounters the rounded belly of a storm lantern in a brass frame. The oily feel of the fuel on his fingers tells him that this is someone's dwelling. He has arrived somewhere; he is dry and there will be light for him here as soon as he finds his lighter in a trouser pocket. When he turns up the flame inside the glass chimney, an astonishing sight is revealed. A simple wall of boards divides off a sheep pen from the living space. He is in the latter, which is arranged around a cast-iron stove.

By way of furniture it contains a bedstead with a straw mattress, the table, two chairs and a stool. There is a supply of dry wood. At the rear of this area a squat fig tree is growing, its uppermost branches sticking through a large opening in the metal roof. Curiously, there is no moisture around the tree. Gazing towards the uppermost branches he can see his shadow, which is cast on a vault coated with some chalky deposit. The sheepfold has been built under an overhang in the rock.

He decides to lay out his sleeping bag at the base of this fig tree, which grows at the entrance to what seems a kind of grotto. He lights a fire in the cast-iron stove, which, to judge by the warmth remaining in its layer of ash, was used only a few hours before. He stretches out at the foot of the fig tree and immediately sinks into a slumber which for once spares him the recurrent picture of the head.

In the morning, he is awakened by a sudden noise. It takes him a few seconds to figure out the source of the din: the frost is causing the metal roofing over the shelter to contract with a sinister cracking sound. Stiff and thirsty, he sits up on his bed and glances through a line of faint light shining between the roof and the sheepfold's front wall, which supports the roof beams.

The sun is coming up over the Rhodope Mountains in Bulgaria, directly to the east, in the direction he is heading. Looking around, he sees a few objects that must have remained invisible during the evening but now emerge in the strengthening light: a small coffee pot, a packet of matches, a gas ring and a box of sugar, all rusty, arranged on shelves in crevices of the rock. Beside the door stands a can of olive oil; a yellow waterproof coat is hanging from a nail just above it, and a shepherd's staff leans against the wall. It is carved out of green wood, and doesn't look like the traditional shepherd's crook: it is straight, with no handle, its top carved in the shape of a pine cone. He decides to take it with him.

Outside, dazzled, he returns directly to the immediate problems of making his way. He had left his point of departure only a few hours ago, and is already tending to consider everything past and gone. The severed head falling off, Christina: it all seems far off, remote.

At this moment he can't deny that he has slept at the foot of a fig tree inside a shepherd's cabin built under an overhang in the rock. But it so happens that the snow has stopped falling, and it looks as if the sun will come up in a cloudless sky. And then there are fields streaming with meltwater, and a thin mist hanging level with his boots above the melting snow. Time and distance will provide him with an explanation for the end of his relationship with Christina. But will he ever discover the identity of that man decapitated by the axe?

A sound of tinkling bells makes him turn his head. He can't see any sheep, but he does notice a pickup parked at the side of a road cut into the mountainside, one storey above the rocks overhanging the fold. Something tells him that he will have to speak to this man who is collecting his flock above. He can see him herding his sheep into a terraced field. The young man, wearing an army jacket and jeans, opens a wooden gate. Nikos can hear his shouts and whistles. The shepherd is talking to his sheep.

He would need to get away very quickly. But Nikos lacks the strength to move; he knows that the man has seen him and will question him. Maybe his picture has already been on TV. It was only to be expected. So he sits down on a large stone in front of the fold. He rests the staff, his newly acquired walking stick, across his knees. He closes his eyes and waits, immersed in the tinkle of sheep bells. He waits for the voice that will eventually address him, for the questions he will soon have to answer. Naturally he'll be obliged to explain what he is doing there, why, and where he is heading. Resigned, he awaits the greeting. He is startled to hear the man say, "I can tell you the GPS location of the fold." The man, who is very tall, is standing in front of him, his sunlit face obscured by the warm steam of his breath when he speaks. He is holding a mobile phone which he consults as he glances at Nikos without a hint of curiosity.

The shepherd reads off, "N 41.15652 E 24.63678."

"That's our position?" asks Nikos.

"No," the other answers, "it's the precise location of the fold. So, if you like, it's where we are, except that very soon we won't be here any longer, but its position won't have changed."

'A crackpot,' thinks Nikos, without uttering a word.

"Pick up your things and come with me," says the shepherd, smiling at him.

"And why should I go with you?"

"Because you must be lost, so that makes you my guest, and anyway there's nothing more for you here, or for me either. And you must be hungry, too."

"All right, I get it, I've slept in your sheepfold and I apologize; I was overtaken by the snow and didn't know where to find shelter."

"Let's go!"

"I'd rather walk."

"My name is Sezan. Come with me."

Nikos doesn't answer; he pulls his bag to him from the low wall on which it was resting, gets up, and goes to close the door of the fold.

"Leave it open, and don't forget your stick."

"I found it here."

"It's yours."

What follows is no longer part of the trajectory imagined by Nikos. He finds himself sitting reluctantly in a red pickup driving downhill towards the Thracian plain, robbed of his route, and along with it the memories that would inevitably have surged up at some turn in a path – like, perhaps, if he'd taken the time to pass through them, the olive groves that now flit past his field of vision, or the sudden silence of the ferry in the humid dawn over Chania harbour, then crossing a gorge on the arch of an old Ottoman bridge, or, even more precisely, the sudden absence of vibration in the ship's cabin, with the engines stopped, his body still not believing the rolling of the ship had ceased, and then the long minutes of nothingness before the docking was announced over the loudspeaker; places along his way, and reliving the disembarkation in Crete with Christina and their children, children of their own, with sleepy faces – a clear impression that must have occurred to him, who knows why, on hearing the noise made by footsteps in the run-off from the melting snow, those stages skipped, leaving nothing for now or the future but a few fragments of a landscape seen through a windscreen, and the pain of losing Christina suddenly reawakened.

The shepherd, whose name he has already forgotten, is driving him to Xanthi, "the town", he said, as if it couldn't be anywhere else: "We're going to the town."

Then, the first question at last: "Where are you going like that?"

"I'm walking the path of the Ancient Way."

"The Ancient Way? You mean the Egnatia Odos?"

"That's it."

"Let me guess, you're an archaeologist, aren't you?"

"Yes, in a way. I'm trying to trace history."

"There's not much of that road left."

"Yes, but in the places where the Ancient Way has disappeared we know where it went."

"So that's why you're walking all alone in the mountains in the middle of winter?"

"Yes."

"I don't know a lot about archaeology. I graduated from the Polytechnic, I'm an engineer. But I've seen bits of that road, the Egnatia, and I remember seeing its route on a map in a book at school."

"You're not really a shepherd, then?"

"I'm becoming a shepherd. I was fed up with city life, and anyway there's no work, because of the crisis."

"I see."

"And archaeology pays well?"

"It all depends."

Nikos comes up with a sum, he gives a few banal details, mentioning the German Archaeological Institute in Athens. The lies come easily, for he is simply repeating what Christina had once told him: "As soon as you begin to remove the soil, you're disturbing the work of years. Layer by layer, painstakingly, slowly, respectfully, I finally discover fragments that once fitted together – an origin. To understand the beginning, you must start from nothing. My job is to deny the human landscape its claim to forget."

He must have fallen asleep and dreamed he saw a patch of snow still lying in a hollow – or he thought that was what it was, but now he realizes it was a town blotting the plain: a blotch of white, for that was its only colour. He opens his eyes a first time, still seeing the pictures of the winding road and the river bridges, the sagging mountain peaks; he is dozing in the shepherd's pickup, which bumps over a railway crossing, and then? Nothing. Nikos has fallen asleep again as Sezan drives along the sandy bank of the Nestos and enters Xanthi. Nikos doesn't see the police roadblock at the edge of the town, just beyond a recently constructed bridge. The four-by-four avoids it, taking a dirt road lower down used by peasants returning at nightfall to their neighbourhoods in this sizeable provincial town. Seeing the police cars blocking the avenue leading to the town centre, Sezan frowns, believing it is some new humiliation being practised on the Turkish-speaking minority. Just as the shepherd accelerates his truck to climb a low embankment and return to the road, leaving the fields behind and slipping into the late-afternoon flow of vehicles in front of the service stations, Nikos awakens fully, with his hands crossed on his legs, which have gone numb, and his face leaning against the window, suddenly encumbered by the appearance of his reflection in the glass. As they drive along a narrow one-way street deprived of sunlight, he hears someone say: "We've arrived." Sezan invites him home for coffee, after which he is welcome to eat with the family and spend a night or two on the living-room sofa – whatever he likes; anyway, there's room for him, and blankets, but Nikos replies, "No thanks, there's no need. I'd rather spend the night in a hotel and start out again on foot tomorrow, but as for the coffee, thanks, with pleasure."

But then he wants to take a short walk and starts to say, "I'm going for a bit of a walk, you can drop me here, yes, in this street with no sunlight," though he didn't say "street with no sunlight", but just asked the shepherd to drop him off in front of an apartment building adorned with washing hung out to dry but failing to do so. They'll meet later because right now, yes, he'd like to walk for a bit, so that he can say he arrived in Xanthi just as he'd imagined it, step after step, abiding by his decision to always keep moving east.

"I can drive you," offers the shepherd, who doesn't understand. Nevertheless, he parks his four-by-four on the pavement and looks at him, watching him search for his bag on the back seat and surely telling himself that this individual is a bit odd.

The shepherd says, "See you on the square at six!"

Out in the damp air, Nikos starts walking; the street, darkened so much by apartment buildings, bristles with balconies on which nothing will dry. Some of them have been converted into verandas enclosed by non-reflecting windows of plasticized aluminium.

Head and shoulders above the column of cars advancing at a snail's pace, with Sezan's pickup still behind him, he plunges into the shade of the ground floors into which high-ceilinged shops are incorporated, and forges ahead under lines of neon lights, avoiding concrete pillars, passing between glued laminates, brushing against new plastering, re-puttying, synthetic resin oozing, for everywhere they are patching up, rewiring, reapplying self-adhesive strips, welcome to Xanthi, to do-it-yourself Greece, a screwed-together Greece, a storehouse of globalization, a country for sale on the ground floor, sold off, the upper floors housing the Greece of below and now evicted onto the street, prostrate, in Xanthi like in Patras, in Koukaki like in Patissia, in Larissa, Greece going for a song, everything cleared out! Bundles of laundry; buckets; plenty of water; bleach "made in"; ladders; cans of oil; washers, leaking; chlorine; balls of string "made in"; shears "made in"; padlocks "made in"; cushions "made in"; folding chairs "made in"; mobile storage cabinets "made in"; flowerpots; waxed tablecloths; rubber boots; pocket lamps; coffee sets; draughts games; tent canvas; saucepans; peelers; rubbish bags; fruit baskets; oil-filled radiators; batteries; carpets; Greece; China.

In Xanthi, in this street devoid of sunlight, the smells linger on, he tells himself, breathing the aromas of a *psistaria*, whiffs of kebab stuffed with white onion, the sizzling fat of tavernas that have never been as empty and gleaming with dreary poverty, cheerless meals around the edge of Xanthi's main square and its marble fountain, its concrete paving stones securely seated as if to make people forget the fractured alleyways that fade into a wasteland, a deserted fairground where a skinny old nag stands silhouetted between two cars, nibbling on a few sparse blades of grass.

On the face of the big clock, an absurdly triumphant folly erected to commemorate… to commemorate what?

And what if he went, if he climbed it to see – to discover what the road to the Bulgarian border is like? He still has time to see dusk fall from the slopes of the Rhodope Mountains onto the tiled roofs of the old town; he has time, before the damp from the Nestos takes over.

Go ahead, take the steps up the alleyways four at a time, stepping on the disjointed stones where the foot rolls over tiny black fossils, the hardened droppings of passing goats vanished forever behind the worm-eaten doors of leprous stables.

Nikos wasn't mistaken. Where the town now meets the mountain road at the edge of a ravine-furrowed forest, it is five o'clock; up there, his gaze can slide unobstructed across the jumble of roofs before reaching the plain beyond, which seems darkened by the river.

Just then the evening bell rings out, grave strokes of the Angelus, as if hurrying to finish. Then silence, the Orthodox church in the foreground, its dome above the stuccoed choir swelled by the amber reflection of the setting sun.

Squatting, arms clutching his knees, Nikos waits. Half German, half Greek, he waits to hear the other call: now it pours from the muezzin's throat, hoarse modulations coming from the loudspeaker on the minaret.

Along with darkness, a sooty smell of woodsmoke rises over the roofs. In the narrow streets of the old Ottoman town, shadows are lengthening under the blank gaze of the corbels. No light testifies to even a silent presence around the table on which a lentil soup awaits. He must return to the square and its bright café signs to believe in the shepherd's invitation, "You'll come and eat with us." And indeed Sezan is waiting there, smiling broadly, holding out a can of beer, the four-by-four's engine running, its door open. Its radio is throbbing with the heavy bass of a *çifetelli*. Nikos accepts a hand-rolled cigarette and doesn't refuse the beer; Greek words come to his lips, leaving a froth that dries in the corners of his stammering mouth.

As they drive, there is no more to be said than before. The paved surface of the square with the clock might open under their feet, the landscape might collapse, they would be there; the streets might be engulfed by the dark of the abandoned stone houses, but the exchange remains inarticulate as the sweet taste of tobacco dispels any obligation to find words, the bitter tang of the beer fills his stomach with contentment, and the heater warms his icy feet.

At Sezan's, in the greyish glow of the neon bulb, Nikos sits on one of the four sofas upholstered in a floral pattern. A synthetic wool blanket for the night is folded on the wooden arm. It will be impossible for him to go and spend the night in a hotel.

On the glass-topped table a couple of vases holding plastic flowers sit on embroidered place mats. To make room for the meal, the shepherd's youngest daughter places them on top of the TV that stands on a glass-fronted cabinet where the framed portrait of an elderly gentleman with a long moustache and wearing a black shirt occupies pride of place among the family photos. His hands rest on a cane identical to the one Sezan gave him that morning.

"It's the same one?" asks Nikos.

"No, not the same, but it was my grandfather who taught me to carve them out of softwood."

"And he's still alive?"

"No, he's dead, *inshallah!*"

Sezan's wife and three daughters don't eat with the men. They serve the olives, the goat's cheese, the egg-and-lemon soup, the *pastourma*, the cucumber salad, the gherkins, the sweet peppers, the beer and the raki. They eat the same meal, but in the kitchen. Their laughter penetrates the cloud of smoke in the living room and tempts the gaze to steal a glance, trying to see what the women's quarters are like, and Nikos is just wondering what the cause of their merriment can be when a brother arrives, followed by a neighbour, then another brother – the youngest, just back from Germany, a student in Berlin, who refuses the raki with a frown: the bearded brother who speaks only the dialect and says, "*As-salaam 'alaikum.*"

Since he is able to reply, "*Wa 'alaikum as-salaam,*" the brother from Germany finally meets his gaze with a questioning, somewhat ironic look. Sezan had judged him capable of this sudden seduction brought about by the greeting and raises his glass, exclaiming, "*Geia mas,* health, good health!" The women's laughter from the kitchen is twice as loud; the youngest daughter has cleared the plates away and emptied the ashtrays, and the black tea arrives, followed by a plate of pastries. The newcomers' questions finally issue from mouths full of honey and almonds – they are crisp, they explode, sticky and twisting.

Nikos is trying to say something like: But why should identity in Islam be expressed by the existence of women who laugh only in the kitchen but not at the table? And Ankara is trying to make use of you to influence Greek domestic policy, isn't it?

He would rather say, But why did we part, Christina, my love? And where did I see that severed head before? It wasn't me, I swear! I wasn't the one who killed him!

Nikolaus Strom protests, 'It wasn't me!' Yet it was him, for the brother has turned on the TV, and it's certainly him, Nikolaus Strom, his name spelled out by the scrolling text, yes, it's he, Nikos, it's his face he sees, his picture in a little window in a corner of the screen. A uniformed police officer is speaking very quickly, followed by shots of the frontier, of the River Evros. Along with Sezan and his family, neighbours and brothers, he reads: "Nikolaus Strom, a German national, wanted for espionage."

'For espionage? Not for murder, for espionage...?' Nikos's head is spinning. He doesn't understand.

In the living room, the conversation has died away. There remain only the sound of the television and pictures of the Evros, photos of a sample of the overpriced wall, of the barbed-wire wall for which the Greeks are about to pay an exorbitant cost: 'Not my wall! The fence I offered them cost much less, half the amount!'

The brother from Berlin has stopped smiling; the others stand up and take their leave. Sezan turns to him. "You're my guest for tonight. But tomorrow you must go."

Nikos has no idea how many hours he has walked today. Sitting on a plastic chair in front of a service-station shop, somewhere in the hills between Komotini and Alexandroupolis, he knows only he's not going to walk one kilometre farther. The crossing into Bulgaria is too risky.

There are police everywhere. He has already skirted two roadblocks by leaving the road and cutting across fields. He has taken a decision: he'll try to cross the Evros into Turkey, at a spot where he'll be least expected. His legs are weary, and but for the icy cascade of the light above his head he would doze off in front of the petrol pumps. He'll find someone to offer him a lift to the next exit from the Egnatia Odos, along the route he had resumed that morning after saying goodbye to the shepherd, who had insisted on driving him all the way to Komotini, where he'd said he had business.

Sezan, the shepherd-engineer, hadn't informed on him. He'd taken an enormous risk by picking him up in his truck. He didn't question him, for Nikos was his guest and accordingly benefited from his complete protection. But now that he is on his own again? Maybe Sezan will phone the police in return for some favour and turn him in? He doesn't think so, but the idea courses through his innards and takes root, growing like a tumour.

He is sitting on his chair in front of the service station, warming his hands on a paper cup of coffee, when he feels a hand on his shoulder. A young man in oil-stained jeans addresses him in broken Greek. He must leave now, the shop is closing, he can't stay. The attendant tells him again that he has no further business here, that he must get up; he must abandon his chair and go on his way.

But, since he doesn't budge, the young man merely shrugs and continues piling up the other plastic chairs.

Inside, a woman turns out the lights and switches two pumps to self-service mode. She shouts something to the young man, who replies that he has already told the man to move on. She leaves it at that. Coming outside, she locks the door and goes off to her little car without another word to the attendant, who is donning a warm coat.

Then he comes over to Nikos and asks if he is all right, if he needs help.

Nikos tells him not to worry, that he's waiting to ask the next person coming in to fill up for a ride to the next exit, to the next town, where he'll be able to find a hotel.

The young man hesitates, and finally says that at this late hour no one will be willing to offer him a lift, that it's unusual to find someone like him sitting that way on a chair, just waiting.

What follows doesn't correspond at all to what Nikos has been told about the migrants who end up in Greece. The attendant, originally from Bangladesh, offers him a bed in his caravan, which is parked on flat tyres in a field beside the filling station.

Nikos says yes, gets up, says he accepts, for he is worn out. He can barely get out the words in Greek, or even English, as he tries to express his thanks in either tongue, one of which the young man apparently speaks fluently.

He has no idea how, but he listens, half-asleep, to the young man's tale. The Europe that had been described to him was nothing like a makeshift home parked alongside a motorway. "But it's not a big deal. At least I'm here, and I can earn something, thanks mostly to the tips I get," he says in his melodious accent.

What follows is the already familiar story, narrated in the words of the young Bangladeshi, of a young man crossing the river Evros. He describes how he crawled between two watchtowers manned by Turkish soldiers to get to the riverbank where the people-smuggler was waiting for him, his voice recounting how no one prevented him from leaving the other side, where there was nothing for him, describing the river-crossing in an inflatable boat, avoiding the floating islands of tree branches as the fine rain soaked through his clothes, and arriving in this new country that is as cold as Turkey, taking his first steps in the Schengen Zone, a long walk through some woods and across boggy ground, and the railway line he was supposed to follow to a little abandoned station where he could collect a little strength before dawn – the time of day when only hope of a better life makes the first hunger pangs tolerable, and when you have to start walking to the Greek town where, they had advised him, it was best for him to go to the police station.

Inside the dark caravan, the story of his crossing continues, so far basically adhering to the route now favoured by the smuggler networks, following the meanders of an apposite discourse that doesn't tolerate the slightest digression: single file, boats, smugglers, abandonment, watchtowers, spotlights, cold water, drowning, guards, dogs, fear, missing landmarks, and the impossibility of turning back.

On the map of eastern Thrace, the course of the river that separates Greece from Turkey is no longer referred to as the Evros, but as a porous border, the main point of entry into the European Union, a sieve, a prohibited military zone, the route to the West, a migratory path. It was across this difficult terrain that the Bangladeshi had ventured, wriggling with all his strength past the barriers of a useless language while refusing to take an iota of interest in the country he is crossing, refusing to see in it any grave obstacle to the more general movement that keeps driving him on, the Bangladeshi relegating the river crossing to a mere springboard, while observers' reports, hostile or sympathetic, wary or supportive, hostile or helpful, exploitative or benevolent, view his journey – the journey of every migrant, illegal or victim – as an odyssey capable of reversing the course of history, of threatening the European Union, of destabilizing Greece.

Unburdened of his story and falling silent in his bunk, the Bangladeshi can let go of the part of him that crossed the Evros – just a few steps in his story, soon to be erased by time.

Turning his back, Nikos falls asleep thinking of his wall, of the wall he represents on this side of the frontier, his wall, the purpose of which is to bar admission to migrants like this Bangladeshi. Listening to the pump attendant has allowed him to recover a rhythm, an entirely impersonal cadence; he has been able to descend into himself, into the depths of memory from which, he feels, forgetting always emerges in the end. At this moment, his story concurs with the migrant's; it does more than coincide with it, for it has become one with his, with his story, theirs, ours, compelled as we are to search for that distant destination where we can sustain our faith in our errant dreams.

Nikos is up at first light. He leaves Macedonia along minor roads, re-entering Thrace across the dry bed of the river Strymon. The Roma is changing a tyre when he sees him. Nikos approaches him slowly, guardedly; the Roma watches him, and points to the spare tyre with his chin. Nikos helps him, and they set off together. Following mostly unpaved little lanes to reach the plain, they head east. But the light is failing and the Roma doesn't want to go any further.

Now Alexandroupolis is in sight on the right; the large building all lit up is the University Hospital. The sound of the Roma's little van fades away. Nikos takes a few steps and stops; he feels that his slow hike has become part of the landscape; then he turns, preparing for the great bend to the north, to above where the Evros enters its delta, traversed by low-flying waterfowl that utter cries of alarm when a migrating bird flies silently by.

At nightfall, he takes refuge in the first village on the outskirts of Alexandroupolis. The hotel seems empty. The receptionist doesn't look up. She is watching television – a Turkish soap opera with Greek subtitles. She must watch all the soap operas, but not the most recent ones. She likely knows nothing of the manhunt.

With his eyes closed in the damp, cold bedroom, he wonders, 'How can one cross a landscape barred by a river: how?'

Days pass, and Nikolaus doesn't seem to be making any progress, possibly because he is thinking a lot and thoughts like his go unremarked, even by him. But tomorrow, for sure, he'll cross the Evros into Turkey. The frontier guards will be too concerned with the migrants to pay attention to someone crossing in a contrary direction.

And even if the Turks are sure to pick him up, it's better to fall into their hands than those of the Greek police. Considering the confusion that reigns on this frontier, it will be easier than entering Bulgaria. And then, above all, while surveying the site for the wall with the Greek army a few weeks before, Nikos had discovered a way to ford the river where it makes an elbow near the base of a watchtower, at a spot where the water is quite shallow. He knows that the guards are relieved at around four in the afternoon. He'll have to see.

Episode VI

From a distance it resembles one of those restaurants found in large Caribbean all-inclusives: a large polygonal roof, little ornamental ponds all around, and little wooden bridges like in a Japanese garden. There is a flagpole at the peak of the roof. This is where Nikolaus Strom was sighted an hour earlier. The man now being questioned is positive; he repeats, "He's the one that was on TV. He was walking on his own towards the river, I saw him go by the windows."

Agent Evangelos notes that the witness was having coffee with his girlfriend when he saw Strom emerge, like a ghost, from the fog. The witness is claiming a reward, and Agent Evangelos leaves Lieutenant Anastasis to explain that there has never been any mention of a reward, and now he is looking at this pastry shop, apparently parachuted onto a plain about fifty kilometres from Alexandroupolis. It is surrounded by a network of dried-up canals and side roads, dotted with little red signs warning of danger: "Landmines!"

'How can that be?' wonders Agent Evangelos. 'Why would Strom decide to return to the Evros region?'

"You're quite sure it was the person you saw on television?" Lieutenant Anastasis asks the witness who, in Agent Evangelos's opinion, is fidgeting too much.

"Yes, I've told you already! And I want the money, it was me that saw the terrorist, me!"

"Who said anything about a terrorist?"

"Why, that guy is one! The guy you're looking for. Give me my money, I'm entitled to it."

Inside the pastry shop, which is set up around a wooden column with plastic windows in its canvas walls, families are ordering generous servings of cream cakes. A queue has formed in front of a vast glass-fronted counter chock-full of pastries adorned with figurines of Santa Claus and chimney sweeps on golden ladders. A priest, leaning towards his children, points to a fruit cake dotted with crystallized fruit. The waitresses speak Bulgarian to one another, and the coffee is very strong.

Outside, the fog is so thick that a superb sense of direction would be required to find the way to the river. Agent Evangelos looks at his watch. It will be dark in five hours. He tells himself it's essential not to lose Strom this time, the way they did in Kavala.

Strom had been spotted for the first time in Samothrace. At this time of year strangers never go unnoticed on those sparsely populated islands. After the description of the wanted man was circulated, at least a dozen people called to say that they were sure they'd seen the man whose picture had been on TV the evening before. Agent Evangelos had found the evidence of a schoolteacher especially convincing. Her description was very precise, and she added that she found the man quite handsome. She even confessed that she sometimes got a bit bored all on her own during the long winters on Samothrace, since there were hardly any visitors, and she'd previously lived in the city. Evangelos had stopped listening to her, for he felt certain that they were on Strom's trail. He therefore issued the order to search all the hotels in Kavala, knowing that the fugitive couldn't have had a chance to rest since leaving the Europa Motel, where he first went to ground after his escape with Polina.

Agent Evangelos takes another look through the window; he can't see anything, but he senses that the frontier is very near.

But why did the fugitive return to the region? 'To tell the truth,' thinks Agent Evangelos, 'I'm not complaining. The directorate wants to arrest him for espionage. He must be crossing a military zone at this very moment. There'll be no need to invent an entire scenario for the prosecution. It's ready-made.'

Lieutenant Anastasis approaches, talking on his mobile, saying, "I think this is it, we have him, he's apparently been spotted approaching the Turkish frontier by a Frontex patrol. In the very north, at the elbow in the Evros. They'll intercept him very soon."

"How's that?" asks Evangelos. "Aren't they sure he's our man?"

"No, but it must be him – a man walking along the riverbank right in the military zone. The patrol's post is on a hill; they picked him up on the infrared radar. The Turks seem to have detected his presence too: the guards on the watchtowers are observing him through binoculars."

The radar! Of course! He'd forgotten the radar!

"But tell me, Lieutenant, what are the colours of the Frontex guys on patrol today?"

"Their colours?"

"I mean their nationality."

"I really don't know."

"You weren't just speaking to them on the phone?"

"No, it was the police station that called. Are you coming, Agent Evangelos?"

"Yes, we're leaving right away, but I want to know which patrol is involved. Call Orestiada back right away, I want to know who's on duty this evening."

The lieutenant is already on the phone, and Evangelos is about to leave the pastry shop when a young man calls out to him – the one who saw Strom, still claiming his reward.

In the mist, the Jeep Cherokee looks like a sunken wreck in a pond. Lieutenant Anastasis is still on the phone; he has sent the witness packing and is holding the phone tucked into his shoulder with his chin; he pulls a face and speaks very fast: "Right away, do you hear?" Agent Evangelos tries to catch snatches of the conversation, he can hear a voice at the other end, someone shouting into the phone; it must be the captain. The jeep's doors slam shut, the engine starts, and they're off. The lieutenant is talking into his on-board radio; he has abandoned his phone for the radio; he is talking to Orestiada, steering with one hand as he insists, repeating, "Right away! Right away!"

Accelerating into the fog, the jeep bounces blindly over the ruts in the dirt road; it tears along, skids, and nearly slides into a ditch barely visible in the yellowish cone of the dipped headlights. The lieutenant drops the receiver and concentrates on the road. Agent Evangelos is hanging onto the strap; he too presses down his foot as if he were driving. Anastasis has turned on the flashing lights, for the jeep has reached the paved road.

Agent Evangelos wants an answer without any further delay; he repeats, "I want to know which patrol is involved."

"The Germans, it's the Germans from Frontex who spotted the fugitive," the lieutenant finally answers.

"Shit! A German patrol arresting a German national; that opens the door to all kinds of problems."

"I can imagine."

The lieutenant is driving his Cherokee flat out; a dense fog passes overhead, turning blue with the reflection of the revolving beam.

"I don't want them to intercept him; Strom is ours, we mustn't let that damn Frontex patrol get to him first."

Lieutenant Anastasis lights a cigarette, draws the cord of the radio receiver to him and calls the police station. He immediately hands the radio to Agent Evangelos, who says, "Captain, is that you, Captain? Captain, you must order the patrol to return to its observation post, yes, yes, that's right, but they mustn't lose sight of him, no, no, not tracking him from a distance, not on the ground, just on the radar."

Agent Evangelos drops the radio, lets out a heavy sigh and says, hoarsely, "Please God, not the Germans."

Lieutenant Anastasis offers him his packet of cigarettes; Evangelos pokes around in it, and the two smoke silently, travelling at a hundred and sixty kilometres an hour on the road that runs next to the river, heading upstream. Outside, the fog hits the doors of the Cherokee, piles up on the bonnet, is shredded noisily by the wheels. 'All this fog coming at the jeep, a grey mass rising over us, it's the Evros frontier finally coming into sight.'

"Agent Evangelos? Agent Evangelos, would it bother you it if I put on some music?"

Lieutenant Anastasis hasn't waited for an answer; he turns on the radio, and just as they reach the village of Tychero, to the music of a Cretan lyre, the Cherokee is going fast, it emerges, still dripping, from the fog, like a plane from the cloud ceiling. Just then Agent Evangelos's mobile vibrates, and Sokratis Retzeptis's name appears on the screen.

No doubt about it, the sun is shining. It would make sense to put down his bag. It would make sense for Nikos to hide out in this room with a view towards the river, which is obscured by a row of tall poplars. At a glance the village seems deserted. Then the bus arrives, stopping on the square; the road runs through its centre, and on it the traffic moves very fast. A girl has got off. Wearing a helmet down over her ears and with her head bobbing, she takes the first street on the right before entering a house with the only cast-iron balcony that overlooks the densely wooded hills rather than the river. A woman coughs somewhere, a rooster crows. In the bus station office, which also serves as a café, a few men are playing *tavli*.

Turkey is just on the opposite bank. Nikolaus can see the red roofs of houses through the trees, but he can't see the river, only guess at its presence.

The girl in the helmet makes him think of other Greek girls, and of one especially – Christina's daughter.

But it's time to cross the Evros. A moment ago he had heard a helicopter and seen several police cars driving along the road. There isn't a minute to lose; he must get off Greek soil.

Nikos leaves the village of Kastanies behind him and makes for the barrier of trees behind which he can see a red flag floating, with a white crescent and five-pointed star. The villages on the banks of the Evros know the conundrum of the river; they still must live with it. The migrants who come ashore one morning are a reminder of the unknown across the Evros. This morning there were five, sitting on the terrace of a café. But the café was closed and they were counting their remaining small change, hoping to complete the journey to the station in Alexandroupolis by bus. A week ago they were in Algiers. The charter flight to Istanbul costs a hundred dollars. The bus fare from Istanbul to Edirne costs twenty Turkish lira. The crossing of the Evros can be negotiated for six hundred dollars.

A bass voice strikes up a chant that levels out over the river, the only material frontier, as the monotonous Orthodox chant overlies the call to prayer from the great

Selimiye Mosque in Edirne. An Orthodox priest is saying Mass somewhere behind him, sheltered by the roof of the little chapel built on a hillock that rises above the plain. He can see the faces of the uniformed guards, incongruous figures adhering flatly to the busy landscape. At the first fork he keeps left, following a little road that traverses some trees before reaching a shallow, turbulent stream. At this spot the water is so low that the road crosses it with no need for a bridge. The two guards have vanished. The helicopter is back. Nikos doesn't bother to look up; advancing across open ground, he reaches the middle of the ford, leaping from stone to stone, indifferent to the cold water that sometimes reaches his knees.

Now he is across; the helicopter clatters somewhere above the trees. On the opposite shore, Nikos starts running, leaving Greece behind. His head is suddenly spinning, it's from fatigue; he has eaten nothing for the past twenty-four hours.

Then Christina's laughter, Christina on the riverbank, calling to him in Greek. Yes, it's really her. No, he won't turn around, it's her ghost, she doesn't exist, she's no longer part of his life, he won't listen to what she's trying to tell him, and anyway he doesn't understand the language, he speaks no Greek, for once and for all. Now he hears only Christina's laughter, carried on the wind, which is mild for the time of year. He is leaving his mother's country behind. In a pile on the riverbank, like luggage too heavy to carry across, he is abandoning his memories, all the contradictions, all the parts of life he has never been able to draw together, and that horrible, grimacing head.

Nikos has crossed the wall; he has crossed his personal wall. His entire story remains in a pile on the riverbank. He has evaded the Greek police and will soon be in the hands of the Turkish army. He'll explain to them, and ask to speak to his embassy.

Once, in Athens as a child, Nikos had approached his Greek grandfather's garden fence. Over the railing he had seen the white dust from the marble works as it settled. It was a time when he spoke both languages, a time when the world was still comprehensible. For a long time he thought he'd gone beyond his great-grandfather's garden fence; for a long time he thought he understood Athens – it was where he was from, and for a long time he believed he was at home there, picking up scraps of his mother's language, all those inscriptions on the city's walls, to continue the story that began when the marble-workers' saws fell silent that day in July 1972, two and a half hours after midday.

Today, let Christina laugh; he is no longer part of her world, he is across the placid river, without a murmur, and he allows forgetfulness to mount inside him. The landscape is becoming blurred, the green of the trees is fading, the sky is tilting. On the shore, Nikos has fallen on his knees.

Christina, why are you laughing at me like that?

On the map of Greece, says Christina, *the river Arda runs in the very north. It rises, like the Evros, in the Rhodope Mountains, and finally flows into the Evros a little way after the village of*

Kastanies, a few metres from the Turkish frontier, just before the fork you took to avoid the Turkish guard post. At that point, as you can see, the road crosses the Arda, and leads to a narrow strip of land that joins up with the Greek bank of the Evros. You'll see the Turkish flag floating over a watchtower on the other side, which will tell you you're not across the Evros. Continue in the same direction and it will lead you to the village of Marasia. Soon you'll find me there, in the square, sitting under a fruit tree with big leaves, at the midpoint between both riverbanks. There's rarely anyone around, as you'll see. People don't like to live on the frontier. But you'll like it, I'm sure. There's a little café, like the ones where we always meet. You're still in Greece, my love.

Nikos's head aches. He opens his eyes. There's no helicopter in the sky any more. His throat is dry, he is chilled to the bone, he has no strength left. He struggles to his feet and takes a few steps, but he has to sit down. Again, he almost loses consciousness; his breathing is shallow. So just like that, he has committed an error. The stretch of river he crossed wasn't the Evros. Now he's done for. He has come up against a wall – especially since he is no longer alone. He sees them straight ahead: a man in his fifties with a short haircut and three days' growth of beard. He is standing there in a large overcoat, leaning against the door of a Jeep Cherokee belonging to the Greek police. The man is watching him, smoking, looking tired. He doesn't seem like a policeman.

The jeep is stopped on some railway tracks, on a level crossing, just opposite the abandoned railway station in

Marasia, a little Greek village jammed in between the Arda and the Evros, on the Turkish border.

Beyond the trees, Nikos can see Turkish sentries moving around on the top of their watchtower. He can make out the colour of the uniforms; the sunlight glints on the lenses of their binoculars.

Yes, they were waiting for him there, on the Greek side of the frontier. Any attempt to escape would be pointless. He stands up and walks towards the jeep. He reaches the man, who jettisons his cigarette. Without a word, he opens the rear door and gestures to him to get in. Inside is another, younger policeman in a black leather jacket. He doesn't turn around, but their eyes meet in the rearview mirror. He seems tired too, but he does look like a policeman. He handcuffs Nikos.

The jeep drives one or two kilometres along the Evros, passing through Marasia. There is no sign of Christina on the village square, and Nikos can see clearly that there is no café.

But now he knows that she was right. Nikos is no foreigner, for when the man asks his name he answers in Greek. And he begins to tell him the whole story in his language, the language he shares with Christina.

It's an extraordinary day for Athens, thinks Agent Evangelos. Outside, far below on Alexandras Avenue, the demonstrators' numbers are swelling. From his office window, on the eighth floor of the GADA, the big cube of glass, asbestos and steel that houses the headquarters of the Attica General Police Directorate, Agent Evangelos observes the crowd. The Metro station at the corner of Panormou Avenue is surrounded by a cordon of blue-uniformed police. The riot squads are on a war footing too – at least four units, a hundred or so men in green fatigues: there are a lot of toughs wearing helmets in the streets today. Agent Evangelos sees them regrouping behind buses with shatterproof windows, carrying their shields. They have been ordered to fire tear-gas cartridges if the crowd makes the slightest breach in the security bar-riers. They will shoot in any case, Agent Evangelos doesn't doubt it for a moment. Just then he reads a single slogan on the banners being unfolded on the avenue: "No Wall!"

Standing there in front of the window, Agent Evangelos is puzzled. This disturbance isn't his problem, but he finds it difficult to comprehend. 'So the spokesman for the Ministry of Public Order and Citizen Protection just had to announce the arrest of a German national in connec-tion with the construction of the wall? Was such a simple announcement all that was needed to stir up so much opposition to closing the frontier to migrants? I'm more surprised than anyone,' Agent Evangelos tells himself, 'though I should have expected that kind of reaction.'

However, a few minutes from now, as planned, Strom will be questioned in this room.

This sudden wave of opposition to the construction of the wall doesn't suit the government. The frontier is a business. Agent Evangelos reflects on power, on the only established power in Greece: he reflects on the power of money, thinking about one of its most influential representatives, a man who wants to control everything, who has foreseen everything – everything, that is, except the re-emergence of the "No Wall!" movement. Yet, there, beneath the windows of the police, the opposition to the wall is growing, swelling, and may very well explode in the face of power. Not that a few days of rioting in Athens are anything to fear. Power doesn't care about the usual list of bus shelters burned or small businesses ruined. From its lofty height, it contemplates the recurrent spasms of the ailing heart of the metropolis, the inevitable confrontations that will end in the nth siege of the Athens Polytechnic, the university sanctuary where photocopiers now spit out almost nothing but pamphlets by the hundreds – an inviolable refuge where the corridors serve as an arsenal for Molotov cocktails. But power fears something entirely different, something taking the form of a more widespread citizen's movement of opposition to the wall, something resembling an international protest.

It seems that French and Italian demonstrators are organizing a sit-in at the watchtowers on the frontier around Orestiada. The Turkish border guards must have a grandstand view. Soon, after Strom's interrogation, Agent Evangelos will call Anastasis. He'll tell the lieutenant: "After the migrants and Frontex, you're going to come across a new species of fauna in the Evros natural reserve: anti-wall demonstrators chaining themselves to a strip of land between Greece and Turkey. Can't you just imagine?" Still by the window, Evangelos hears the first shouts, a dog barking, and sees a liver-coloured dog in front of the riot squads; he recognizes it, always the same one, barking, barking.

Agent Evangelos has placed a document in a transparent sleeve on the desk: Nikolaus Strom's statement. It has already been typed, and awaits only his signature.

His superiors have asked Agent Evangelos to make the situation clear to Strom. "The German must sign it, he has no choice. If he refuses, then…"

"Then what?" asked Evangelos.

"He'll sign it whatever, it's in his best interest, isn't it?"

Yes, Strom will sign all right. But Agent Evangelos will contravene his orders. He will disobey them, for he wants to discover the truth about the severed head; he wants to discover the killer's identity, whether it was Polina or Nikolaus Strom; he wants to know the precise circumstances of Batsis's decapitation. There will be a statement, which he'll take down. 'It'll be up to me – me, Agent Evangelos – to write out the true account of the murder on the Evros. Then, once Strom has finished, I'll place the other document before him, the statement prepared in advance; he will be obliged to read and sign it. The truth will remain between us two, but it will have been established, and I intend to make use of it in my own way. I'll administer justice in my own way, the way it should have been done.'

In a few moments, Nikolaus Strom will enter the room, probably worn down by three nights and three days spent in a permanently lit cell. Agent Evangelos has made sure to soften him up. He wants him to be on tenterhooks, his nerves already frayed. But it's an entirely different person who is brought before Evangelos a moment later; Strom is perfectly calm. He stands there, his features drawn, his eyes brilliant with fever, a man marked by fatigue, but calm, seemingly at peace, as if relieved, greeting him in Greek with a smile, not a defiant smirk – no, a confident smile, the smile of a man who seems to have been looking forward to this moment.

"Sit down! Officer, remove his handcuffs!"

Outside, the clamour of the crowd is rising. A gust of fresh air enters through the half-open window. The officer has closed the door behind him. Agent Evangelos sits across from Nikolaus Strom. He looks at him, he looks at the man and thinks to himself, 'It's true, he's a bit Greek. He's half Greek, I tend to forget that.'

"Do you feel up to speaking Greek? Maybe you'd prefer English?"

"Greek is fine."

"Great! We met earlier, three days ago, but let me introduce myself: Agent Evangelos, from Directorate C of the National Intelligence Service. Do you know why you're here, in this office?"

"Yes."

"Tell me."

"You arrested me in connection with certain events that took place in the Evros region. I didn't kill that individual."

"What individual?"

"I don't understand."

"You say you're not responsible for the death of some person or other. What person are you referring to?"

"But… The man… the man I struggled with —"

"You don't know his name?"

"I know nothing about him, it was night, I had no idea who he was, he jumped on me, and then…"

"You killed him?"

"I don't think so. I wasn't the one who killed him."

"I don't believe you. No one will believe you."

"I didn't kill him, I've never killed anyone."

"You fought with this individual outside the Eros brothel, and ended by striking him with an axe."

"I swear to you, it wasn't me who struck him with the axe."

"You cut off his head, you beheaded Andreas Batsis, born in Piraeus on 9 January 1976."

"It wasn't me, it was —"

"You killed that man with a blow from an axe, why deny the obvious?"

"It wasn't me. It was… It was that girl. She was out of her mind, she had a crazy look in her eyes."

"Now we're getting somewhere! I was sure you'd accuse that poor girl. What do you know about her?"

"Nothing, nothing! I'd never seen her before."

"You didn't know who she was, yet you combined forces with her in disposing of a headless corpse, after which you made your escape together —"

"We were both terrified. I was acting impulsively, on reflex. I saw right away that I was in a situation in which the only solution was to escape. And I felt sorry for the girl. She's a prostitute, she —"

"Keep to the point! I know who the girl is, and I know her story. It's yours that interests me."

"But it was you who asked if I knew who she was —"

"Let's continue. You killed Batsis. The girl, who was completely under the influence of drugs, helped you to move the body and —"

"No, I didn't kill that man."

"Well, that poor girl, for whom you felt such sympathy, is the one who insists it was you who took the axe to the victim."

"I don't understand. Why would she?"

"Now listen to me. I'm going to ask you to go over everything from the start, and I'll take down your statement. I'm going to write out everything you tell me. Please begin with the reasons for your presence in Greece. Tell me why you went to that brothel – the Eros, isn't it?"

"The Eros, yes. But I'd never been there before."

"I don't care. I'm not asking you to justify anything, I'm just trying to establish the facts, do you understand?"

"Yes."

An explosion rings out below, followed by two others. Agent Evangelos gets up, closes the window and sees the demonstrators running to take shelter in front of the football stadium across the road; he sees the riot police charging, batons raised.

"Do you know what's going on outside, down in the street?"

"No."

"Those are the 'No Wall' people."

"The what?"

"Demonstrators shouting 'No Wall! No Wall!' They don't want your wall."

"It's not my wall."

"It could have been."

"I'm sorry, but what happened had nothing to do with the wall."

"How can you be so sure?"

"I was driving along that road and I saw that sign, saying Eros, so —"

"You'll tell me all about that later. So you were in the Evros region to investigate the construction of a wall, isn't that right?"

"I was scouting things out, preparing to offer a surveillance system to the army. That was my job."

"And you thought your wall wouldn't upset anyone?"

"I'm not sure I understand."

"Would you like us to switch to English?"

"No, it's not my language, but —"

"Nikos, may I call you that? Can I call you Nikos, like your woman friend Lazaridou?"

"You talked to Christina? But why? You had no right, she has nothing to do with this business!"

"What business?"

"The wall, the fight, everything! Please leave Christina out of all this."

"You see how everything is connected: your woman friend, the wall, the fight."

"I've told you the truth about that man's death. I'm innocent."

"Okay, that's your version of the facts, I'm taking note of it. What about the wall?"

"I've nothing to say."

"Tell me, Nikos, when did you recognize that you were being led up the garden path by the colonel?"

"I don't know any more. Maybe the day when he failed to turn up for our meeting without calling to explain. But even before that I felt I was being watched. I had a feeling of being very alone, suddenly, just like that. People stopped answering my phone calls. I lost contact with Athens, though everything seemed to have begun on the right foot. I'd made an excellent offer, the colonel and I had checked things out on the frontier, at Nea Vyssa, on the right bank, west of the river, near that triangle of land along the Turkish border."

"The Karaağaç Triangle, as they call it on the other side. Now, tell me how you ended up in that brothel... By the way, if I'm using a typewriter, it's because we haven't got a spare computer. Mine isn't working just now, and we're poorly equipped – the crisis, you know. Maybe you've heard about it?"

Nikolaus Strom is holding his head in his hands. Outside, it sounds like a war. The detonations from the tear-gas guns shake the windowpanes; the roar of the crowd is rising; it reaches the eighth floor of the GADA building and enters the office of Agent Evangelos, who is sitting at his typewriter.

"You'll sign the statement once we've heard your entire confession."

Confession of Nikolaus Strom, born 21 April 1971 in Hamburg. Office No. 78, GADA, Athens, 7 January 2011.

Interrogation conducted by Agent Evangelos of Division C of the National Intelligence Service.

In May 2009, Nikolaus Strom submitted a bid to the Greek Ministry of Defence for the construction of a wall along the river Evros.

In the past, Strom had already sold security systems for use in frontier zones in Israel and Turkey, in south-eastern Anatolia.

He defended the quality of his bid, making two excellent arguments: his experience, and an unbeatable price. According to Strom, the budget announced by the Greek government, which at the time was seeking European financial assistance to build the wall, was extremely inflated.

Strom believed that his Greek descent through his mother would work in his favour.

As soon as his bid reached the Ministry of National Defence it was studied by the high command of the Greek Armed Forces. Colonel Alecos Papadopoulos, of Frontier Security, took personal charge of the file. Strom's bid, which was considered interesting, underwent an initial assessment that resulted in a recommendation to pursue it further, as was communicated in a letter addressed to Strom's residence in Athens.

Following his initial communications with Colonel Papadopoulos, which were never by email but always via telephone, Strom visited the Evros region on two occasions between 2009 and 2011.

On 1 December 2010, Strom was invited by Colonel Papadopoulos to carry out an initial survey of the site, in the commune of Orestiada, along twelve and a half kilometres of land frontier. This meeting took place, and Nikolaus Strom obtained a verbal assurance from the colonel that a contract would be signed. Subsequently, however, Strom lost all contact with the colonel, who became unreachable and failed to attend a second meeting arranged to take place in Orestiada on 17 December 2010. Distraught, Strom remained in the region attempting to contact the colonel, without success. During this entire period, but especially on the days preceding the scheduled meeting with Colonel Papadopoulos, Strom sensed that he was being followed.

On 20 December 2010, Nikolaus Strom received a phone call from Colonel Papadopoulos arranging to meet that evening in a "bar" situated alongside National Road E90, just outside the village of Didimoticho in the direction of Orestiada. The colonel claimed that this was the most discreet location in which to discuss the proposal, adding that the premises were secure and under his control. Strom therefore rented a car and followed the Colonel's instructions.

When he arrived, he noticed a neon sign advertising the Eros brothel. Looking for the entrance, he walked around the building, which was poorly lit, and stumbled into some sheets hung out to dry. At that moment a light went on and he saw a terrified young woman who seemed to be escaping from something or someone. She was holding an axe, as if to defend herself. When he stood up and told her she had no reason to fear him, she brandished the axe and began shouting.

Seeing that the girl was "terrified", as he put it, and feeling threatened by the axe, Strom stepped to one side and grasped the young woman's arm, at which point she dropped the axe.

A man came on the scene. He attacked Strom, throwing him to the ground. Strom resisted, struggling with the unidentified man, who attempted to strike him with the axe. The young woman then kicked the unknown man in the back, allowing Strom to free himself. The axe had fallen to the ground again. Picking it up, the girl delivered a heavy blow to the neck of the assailant, who was attempting to get to his feet. The man collapsed, and blood spurted out, for his head was almost severed from his body.

In their panic, Strom and the young woman joined forces to carry the corpse along a dirt path. In this process, the head became detached from the rest of the body.

Strom and the girl then made their escape on foot. They finally reached a small, deserted railway station. Nikolaus Strom explained to the terrified girl that they had to wait. Retracing his steps, he found his car. But before reaching the car park he discovered that the body had disappeared. Only the head remained, farther up the path, near the brothel. He recognized the man's face; he had seen those features somewhere before.

On reaching his car, Strom put his bloodstained jacket in the boot and drove to the hotel in Orestiada, where he changed his clothes and settled his bill. He then found another hotel on the outskirts of the village, the Hotel Europa, and went back to fetch the girl. They spent twenty-four hours in this hotel room. The girl was panicking. Strom did not know what to do. The next day he told her he was going to buy each of them a warm coat and hire another car. He planned to leave the region, drive to Thessalonica and enter the Republic of Macedonia.

In Orestiada, Strom observed that there was considerable activity around the police station. He encountered several patrol cars, and did not dare to rent a car. He began by hiding his vehicle in a wooded area near the river, and burned the bloodstained coat that was still in the boot. By the time he returned to the Europa Hotel on foot, night was falling. He regretted having brought the girl along, for she seemed most unresourceful, though he now admits that he was afraid that she would go to the police and tell them everything.

When he reached the hotel room, the young woman had disappeared. Overcome by fear, he packed his bag and walked to the bus stop farthest from the town centre. He took the first bus to Alexandroupolis. It was then he realized that he had left his mobile on the bedside table in the Hotel Europa.

The following day, Strom took time to reflect. Telling himself that the police must already be looking for him, he tried to cover his tracks and avoided major roads. After spending three days hiding in Alexandroupolis, he decided to travel to Kavala by way of Samothrace. He thought that in Kavala he would have a safe hiding place in the Imaret Hotel, where he had stayed as a guest in the past, and where he hoped no one would think of looking for him. When the police came to search the hotel, he managed to make his escape on foot. He planned to cross into Bulgaria and go to the German Embassy in Sofia.

Directorate C of the National Intelligence Service
Report of 7 January 2011 – GADA-ATH
File No. ZYAXB-28265-10

Written statement of Nikolaus Strom, national of the Federal Republic of Germany. Interrogation conducted by AE in GADA, 07/01/11

BORN: 21 April 1971, Hamburg, Germany
NATIONALITY: German (Father – Hans Strom, 1938);
    Greek (Mother – Melina Tsaltas, 1946)
MARITAL STATUS: Single
PROFESSION: Salesman
INTERROGATION OF THE ACCUSED: 3 January 2011/
    Nea Vyssa military zone/Orestiada/Evros
    Administrative Unit
DETENTION: Isolation Cell – GADA-ATH,
    03/01/11–07/01/11

STATEMENT OF NIKOLAUS STROM

I acknowledge that I visited the Evros region on two occasions, between 2009 and 2011, with the objective of gathering technological and security data.

I acknowledge that on 3 January 2011, I illegally entered a Greek military zone, on the territory of Nea Vyssa, Commune of Orestiada, Evros Regional Unit.

I acknowledge that on 3 January 2011 I ignored the signs forbidding access to the above military zone.

I acknowledge that on 3 January 2011 I photographed military installations, such as watchtowers, cameras and access roads.

I acknowledge that on 3 January 2011 I photographed the technology of a barbed-wire wall intended to secure 12.5 km of frontier between Greece and Turkey.

I acknowledge that on 1 December 2010, I abused the trust of Colonel Alecos Papadopoulos, who knew nothing of my true intentions, having been informed that I was a journalist reporting for the *Frankfurter Allgemeine Zeitung*. During a press tour of the military frontier zone organized by the Greek army I recorded his words without his knowledge and illegally took a series of photographs.

I acknowledge that, under the cloak of my own commercial activities, which are related to military security, I attempted to assemble as much economic information of a political or commercial character as possible, including proprietary technological, financial and commercial data, in addition to government information, all of which were liable to contribute directly or indirectly to increasing the productivity and improving the competitiveness of German industry.

I acknowledge using or seeking to use illegal, clandestine, coercive or deceptive means to obtain economic information.

I hereby plead guilty to the charges of economic and industrial espionage on behalf of German industry and with the complicity of the Federal Republic of Germany, under the aegis of various private companies acting directly on behalf of German intelligence, starting with my own company, Security Fence Material GmbH.

Signed: Nikolaus Strom

Agent Evangelos leans over the top of his tiny desk, saying nothing more. Elbows on the desk, he observes Nikolaus Strom reading and rereading the statement. Outside, the noise of the demonstration has moved away, and the clean-up trucks are already at work on Alexandras Avenue. At this moment, the battle with the riot police must be raging in the Exarcheia district.

He observes Nikolaus Strom, whose face gives no hint of surprise.

"So?"

"What happens if I don't sign?"

"The question is superfluous, Nikos."

"I was just asking out of curiosity," says Nikolaus Strom, picking up the pen from the desk.

"Just sign! Once you've done that, I'll explain a few things."

Nikolaus Strom signs. He signs, and looks at Agent Evangelos with the same peculiar expression as when he entered the office an hour before.

Agent Evangelos verifies the signatures, asks him to initial two pages at the bottom, watches him as he does so, and senses Nikos's weariness, his enormous fatigue.

"Good! Now listen. To answer your question, if you

had refused to sign I would have done everything in my power to make you do so. I'd have told you that you didn't have any choice, that the alternative was to go on trial for Batsis's murder."

"I wouldn't have believed you. Otherwise, why would you have offered me an arrangement like that? It's in your interest to keep that man's death secret. My guilt is of no interest to you."

"No," answers Agent Evangelos. "but the truth *is* of interest to me. Your confession was essential, as far as I'm concerned. I don't think you killed that man. I believe you; you didn't lie to me."

"This business about spying is ridiculous. No one will believe it."

"You prefer the story about a businessman who decapitates a man in front of a brothel in the open countryside three kilometres from the Turkish border, with a hooker as his accomplice?"

"You just said that you believed in my innocence."

"Anyway, you've signed."

"What's going to happen to me now? And the girl? Will she be tried for murder?"

"At this very moment, she must be moping somewhere in Moscow. There won't be any trial for Batsis's murder."

"You already released her?"

"That murder is of no interest to anyone. And you'll be tried for espionage by a military court. The affair will create an uproar; the finger will be pointed at Germany."

"Germany? I don't understand. And why a military court?"

"You are accused of espionage, Nikos. Merkel will have her knickers in a twist when she's told that a German national was wandering about in a prohibited military zone on the Greco-Turkish border, in possession of memory cards with tons of photographs of the security installations."

"You know I'm not a spy! Germany, as you say, will be able to prove my innocence."

"Maybe. But whoever invented that fairy tale knows what he's doing, and it's in Greece's interest."

"Who are you talking about?"

"Let it drop! For as long as your trial lasts, Germany will be in a position of weakness. And then, to start with, the facts are that you're a German, that you've shown an excessive interest in the Greek frontier – and may I remind you that you were in fact arrested in a military zone?"

"Why such a scenario?"

"Don't complicate things. Just be satisfied with the spy story, and take what comes. You're getting off easily, after all."

"Is that all?"

"No, you know as well as I do that it's a matter of politics. Germany will exert pressure, and Greece will make a gesture."

"And the wall will be built in the meantime, won't it?"

"Ah, now you're beginning to see the light!"

"A Greek wall, built by Greeks."

"The costliest wall."

"The costliest wall, built with European funds."

"Yes, Nikos. But tell me, did you ever discover the name of your rival?"

"My rival?"

"The individual who was awarded the contract for the wall."

"No, but it must be someone influential."

"Yes, someone extremely influential."

Epilogue

My name is Evangelos Montzouris. I was born in Athens, on 14 December 1952. I don't know what came over me, but tonight I decided that from now on I would be the one telling this story, though until a moment ago I wouldn't have sworn it. When I arrived at my office on Alexandras Avenue in the late afternoon, nothing was further from my mind. But by the time I turned out the light, at nine that evening, I understood that I mustn't weasel my way out of things any more. To start with, I went for a beer at the Batman, in Neos Kosmos, on the other side of town, where I'm a regular. I was at the bar when my mobile vibrated in my pocket. It was my daughter. I went out into the street to answer, for the music was too loud inside.

"Dad," Andromeda told me, "you know, I've given a lot of thought to this."

"To what?" I answered.

"To the little one's first name. I think I'm going to break with tradition."

"But that's excellent, Andromeda."

"You think so?"

"Yes, I don't know what your mother thinks about it, but I doubt she'll be upset if you don't give the little one her maternal grandmother's first name. And since the other grandma is no longer with us…"

"I'm glad you understand, Dad."

"Are you surprised? Aren't I partly responsible for bringing you up like that?"

"Yes, you're right. But I wanted to know if maybe you had a suggestion about what to call her."

"Me? It's nice of you to think of that, Andromeda, but it's up to the two of you to choose. Your husband must have a preference."

"Yes, he wants to call her Natasha, but I don't like it; and anyway, I think it's the name of one of his old girlfriends."

"I see."

"So?"

"So what?"

"What name would you give her?"

I answered with no hesitation, "Zoë, 'Life', that's what I'd call her!"

And I think she liked that a lot. She sent me a text message to tell me that her husband rather liked the suggestion too.

Then I went into the bar to get my coat, and set off on foot. I came to Kallirois Avenue, crossed at the lights to the island with the Fix building, and then along Syngrou Avenue, to Falirou Street.

There was something in the air, I don't know what, but I felt on top of the world. Moisture was seeping everywhere, the camber of the road gleamed in the semi-darkness like the back of a black caiman on the surface of a stagnant pool. I can't say why, but what I could see on Falirou Street told me that I had nothing to blame myself for. I went past an old garage with a pointed roof, like a castle straight from the early days of the combustion engine in Athens. The traffic, in fact, wasn't moving this evening, though it's true there's nothing surprising about that when it's parked along the street. But how can I put it? Seeing the cars quite still, as if they were in no hurry to be driven again, their dark bodywork absorbing the orange rain that was falling slowly under the street lights: that was the precise image that made me think I could start to write.

The fact is, I was walking through a desolate streetscape, but inwardly I was elated. I greeted No. 60, the century-old house I'd forgotten about, standing neglected among the post-war apartment buildings, a leprous bourgeois lady of poisonous beauty. The farther I walked along Falirou Street, the deeper became my sense that this was where I was from. I felt it most acutely in front of No. 42 with its mutilated garden, its palm tree triumphant over its sawed-off trunk that pokes out from the neoclassical debris.

Music poured from No. 47, where a salsa school now occupies the two top floors, its windows wide open this evening. I could hear the music, but I didn't listen to it; I was walking under a moonless sky, and told myself that whatever happened never has the meaning we usually attribute to things. I thought especially of my military service under the Colonels.

Sitting at my table I reflect too on my work as an intelligence agent employed by interchangeable ministries, on this democratic regime in which terrorized political families who are always on the defensive succeed and resemble one another. I think about all that, and I can find no plausible explanation for it apart from the ceaseless movement that carries me along and is leading me to the present moment on Falirou Street, sad and chaotic but beautiful as well, head held high despite the poverty, dignified in its filth, a nocturnal trajectory which brings me back to the city where, this evening, I am being reborn.

And if by some chance as I go along the Alpha Bank's icy exterior my way seems a dead end, I carry on, stepping out, and find myself almost at home, at the intersection with Veikou Street. I live a little farther up, on Makriyanni Street (named after one of our heroes, a man of war and of letters whose military feats have marked our history, which exists only rewritten in his new prose). I can see my apartment building opposite, reflected in the windows of the Acropolis Museum. In the evening I sometimes await the moment when the guard turns out the lights in the gallery where the Parthenon friezes slumber. Looking at it every morning, I come to doubt its presence above on the rock.

I recall Lazaridou's face, the Athenian woman I questioned recently, Nikolaus Strom's lady friend. There's nothing to add to this bizarre story apart from her face, which remained completely blank when I told her that her Nikos would be tried for espionage. She didn't believe it. She knows he's innocent. Theirs is an innocent love.

I didn't tell Strom that in a way he owed it to Barbaros that the charges for Batsis's murder were dropped. Initially, of course, Barbaros was bent on eliminating him. When he found out that a German was trying to make the Greek government an attractive offer for the construction of a security wall, he lost no time in creating obstacles for him. His first step was to get Strom involved with one of his trusted henchmen, Colonel Alecos Papadopoulos. He knew he could count on Papadopoulos to put a spanner in Strom's works. And it was also a way to sound out the intentions of this mischief-maker, this potential competitor who had emerged from nowhere. When he understood that the German really did have the potential to snatch the contract for the wall from under his nose, without a moment's hesitation he set about disposing of him. Barbaros is the head of one of the largest industrial groups in the country, with 2,600 employees. His shops have supplied half the Greek population with their mobile phones. This prestigious status doesn't prevent him from having several unsavoury thugs on his payroll; in their eyes he is the fairy godfather who got them out of jail long before they'd served out their official sentences. Batsis, who had been sentenced for the murder of a shipyard worker in Eleusis, had been working for him for years.

Without informing Colonel Papadopoulos of his intentions, Barbaros merely asked him to arrange a false meeting with Strom at the Eros, a spot near the frontier that could hardly fail to attract his competitor, and where nothing or nobody should have been able to prevent Batsis from dealing with Strom. The police would have considered it an underworld killing: a foreigner murdered in murky circumstances in a brothel on the Turkish border. But the sudden eruption of the terror-stricken Polina, still half-crazed by the hallucinogen administered during the Frontex orgies, had ruined the plan.

When he learned that his hitman was dead, Barbaros grew concerned. The inquiry into Batsis's murder, with all the publicity that would have surrounded it, could well be disastrous for him. Eventually, his name would have been dragged in. So Barbaros decided to pick up his phone. Someone who enjoys his degree of influence finds it easy to contact government ministers, even past midnight. As usual, he was able to obtain a hearing. It was a matter of covering up a murder in the Evros region, he told a powerful individual. The interests of the Greek government, and accordingly of the entire country, were at stake. A decapitation on the strategic frontier zone of the European Union would put Athens in an impossible situation in the negotiations with Brussels to agree to share in financing the wall. His message didn't fall on deaf ears.

There remained the problem of Strom gadding around the countryside and quite likely to mention his links to the colonel. But Barbaros found a way to turn the situation to his advantage. First, the police would have to get hold of Strom. Then they would open his interrogation by accusing him of Batsis's murder. He would certainly deny it and complain loudly about the injustice. But the cards were stacked against him: his presence at the Eros on the evening of the murder, his attempt to hide the victim's body, his flight in the company of a vulgar little Russian whore who'd accused him of decapitating Batsis before her very eyes, and, finally, his attempt to escape from Greece, constituted damning evidence. With Strom in such a weak position they would only need to offer him a deal: if he pled guilty to a charge of economic and industrial espionage, and trespassing in a prohibited military zone, the police would drop the murder charge. Then the media would only have to be brought into the loop, and Germany would find itself, unexpectedly, in an embarrassing position. And for a good reason: one of its nationals had been arrested on the frontier with Turkey. Under questioning by the intelligence services, Strom would finally admit to being employed by German companies hoping to win an exclusive contract of one and three quarter million euros to build a fence to bar clandestine migrants from entering the Schengen Area. Berlin could protest as much as it liked. The espionage case, despite the denials, would weaken the German government and leave it unable to prevent an allocation of European funds to assist the Greeks to construct the security wall themselves. And since Barbaros would be the one to roll out the barbed wire along the frontier, he would end up with the profits. So things had turned out exactly as Barbaros had orchestrated them.

This evening, on Falirou Street, I feel unburdened of my need to learn the truth. Now I know that our existence is just a fiction. Barbaros is a creation, our creation, the creation of us Greeks. It is we who have given birth to this monster who hungers after power and wealth, this man who acts in the shadows, whose invisible omnipotence is our ruination, the ruination of Greece.

But we still have the power to rid ourselves of him, if we really want to…

My motorbike is in its usual place, on what is now a pedestrianized street. I get into the saddle, and for once put on my helmet. In normal circumstances I carry it on my arm; that's how it is. But not tonight. I button my coat, take my pistol from its holster and put it in my belt, where it is easily accessible. It is loaded (I checked again as I was leaving the office).

It takes me a few seconds to reach Amalias Avenue. I get green lights all the way, and I'm already on Syntagma Square, in front of the parliament buildings. A bus from the riot squads is parked on Sofias Avenue, opposite the French embassy. The *evzones*, standing stiffly in front of their sentry boxes, don't bat an eyelid. Now I can feel the moist, freezing air whip my face, but I don't lower my visor. Not yet. At this hour of the night there's not much traffic. It takes me barely eight minutes to reach Ekali.

Now I'm passing through Ambelokopi. My eyes are stinging. The acrid smoke of burning wood floats in mid-air above the lower streets, where it has become too costly to heat homes with oil or electricity. I traverse the well-heeled neighbourhood of Psychiko, the big Hygeia Hospital, and the Olympic stadium, I speed past the monsters of glass and steel planted in the former orchards of Maroussi. In Kifissia, the streets are empty; there are still Christmas decorations on the balconies.

In Ekali, high above the Attic plain, on the only slopes of Mount Pentelikon where trees still grow, silence reigns. People must sleep soundly in these family strongholds. The smell of burning wood is not as acrid here. Smoke from fireplaces spices the mountain air.

I am on the other side of the street, opposite his house, out of range of the CCTV. The gate is closed, but the lights are on. Behind the wall surrounding the property I can see through the laurels that the lights are on throughout the entire house. Near a window there is a sofa and a low table. The master of the house is expected any minute now. His plane landed an hour ago. He is returning from London. His chauffeur went to fetch him from the airport. Barbaros will arrive very suddenly. He will be unsuspecting, and this evening, according to information received, he has no bodyguard.

The gun feels light in my hand. It's odd: I have a sudden feeling of déjà vu. There's also something of that in the writing I've started – as if everything that has happened to me since the evening I was told about the severed head has already been written down. But until now, someone else has told my story for me. From now on, I'll be the one speaking, the one writing in the first person.

That's what he thinks.

Yes, that's what he thinks, because Agent Evangelos's mobile is vibrating in his coat pocket. It's his daughter. Why does she have to call right now? He answers. She is angry with him; they're waiting for him at her house, he's very late as usual, but this time she won't forgive him, so he had better come right away.

Agent Evangelos mounts his bike once more, and heads back into Athens.